A FARMER'S CHRISTMAS

FALLING FOR A COWBOY
BOOK 2

LILLIANA ROSE

BLURB

City girl, Raven, took a chance, the biggest in her life, and moved to Ben's alpaca farm after the Royal Show. Nearly three months later, she's trying to adjust to life on a farm and living with Ben when they hardly know each other. To make the arrangement even more tricky, his mom also lives in the same house with them. Above all, she wasn't prepared for the feeling of isolation that comes with living on the farm.

Ben is enjoying finally being in a relationship, and better still, Raven is living with him. Life couldn't be better, but he's worried farm life might not be agreeing with her. The problem is his commitment to his farm sometimes has to come first. He always thought once he found his soul mate, things would be easy. It's far from that. Will he step up to fight for what he's always longed for?

Christmas will be different for them both this year, more than they could ever imagine with bush fires threatening their livelihood. Will it be too easy for Raven to return to the city and her family? Or will she stand with Ben and fight for a future with him?

Sometimes you need to fight for what matters in your life. No matter what.

A FARMER'S CHRISTMAS

To Kimba,
you daft dog, you!

INFORMATION AND DICTIONARY

This book has been written using US English, but the book's story is set in Australia. Some euphemisms that form part of the Australian spoken word may be used. If you would like further explanation, or to discuss Australia, please do not hesitate to contact the author. Contact details have been provided, for your convenience, at the end of this book.

Bloody – This is an expletive used to intensify or emphasize.

    Ute – A utility vehicle or pick-up.

CHAPTER 1

Friday, December 20th

Laptop under her arm and an instant coffee in the other, Raven hipped the screen door and stepped outside to the morning. The earthy smell of animals and heat hit her nose. After nearly three months of living here, the country scents in the air still assaulted her senses.

Will I ever get used to this?

Ben reckoned she should've by now.

She sighed. Ben. He'd been up and gone this morning well before she'd woken. She wasn't sure how he managed to get out of the bed they shared without waking her. But he did. Every morning. He got up, without fail, to do the morning chores and whatever else that needed to be done. Now, there was the addition of harvesting to add to the workload.

Raven had been completely naïve at what it meant not just to move to the country but also deciding to live with Ben, on his farm, with his mom, Janette.

What was I thinking? She put her computer and coffee on the round wrought iron table under the veranda at the back of the old farm homestead. It wasn't her brain she'd been thinking with, that's for sure.

They'd started seeing each other once a year, a fling, a few days of hot, passionate sex, and somehow a connection began to form between them. One that had led her right here to the country and living with him in what felt like the middle of nowhere. She certainly couldn't see the neighboring farms from where she sat, only the sheds and land that stretched out as far as she could see, scattered with some trees. There was life out there. She'd even met some of the neighbors, so she had proof that she really wasn't alone, but a feeling of loneliness constricted her chest, shortening her breath.

Initially, the plan had been to rent a property in Keith, the nearest town to the farm. It had been the biggest risk she'd taken in her twenty-six years—to move from the city to the country. It had been rash. Exciting. Fun. Daring.

Since she'd lost her job as a graphic designer in Adelaide, she'd decided to pursue her idea of running her own business sooner rather than later. Money was a lot tighter than she realized without a steady income while starting her own business. When Ben suggested she move in with him, she hastily agreed, thinking of how much money she would save and how much fun it would be to have more time with him. They did. To begin with. Then the harvest started, and she'd hardly seen him for the last six weeks.

Raven fluffed the square cushion and put it back on the seat, ignoring that it was too big, and sat down. It wasn't all bad. At least her office arrangement was inspiring.

The backyard stretched out down a rolling hill, the grass green from the bore water near to the house. Then it slowly died out where the water didn't quite reach, more so now that it was summer. It hadn't rained for weeks. This was something she'd hadn't noticed when living in the city. She saw the consequences more living here in the country.

Maybe I'm adjusting more than I realize.

A big orange tree stood proudly to her left, roots deep to reach the water table and survive the summer months. Its branches extended out randomly as it had been left to grow as it pleased over the years. Oranges left over from last season scattered rotting on the ground, the new fruit, small and green beginning to grow. Ben had explained to her that this was a summer orange tree which fruited in late January.

An old shed stood to her right, the wooden paneling falling off, exposing the insides to the light of day, revealing dust and rusty, old farm machinery which hadn't been used for decades.

Rex, the motley colored cat, sauntered up to her and rubbed against her leg, wanting food even though she never had food with her in the morning.

"Good try," she said to him, reaching down, stroking his long body.

Meow. His eyes looked up at her in hope for a scrap or two.

"Not from me."

She opened her laptop and waited for it to boot up. For her, this was an early start to the day. It was just eight o'clock. She was already showered, dressed, and ready to work. Even though it was likely that the only persons she would see today were Janette, and hopefully Ben, unless he came in very late as he had done a few times, Raven had taken the time to do her hair, tied it back into a messy bun, and wore long, loose linen pants with a flowing light pink sleeveless top. What she hadn't bothered with was makeup. It had felt a little odd at first not putting on foundation, eye shadow, blush, and mascara, almost like she was stepping out showing her real self to the world, not that anyone was around to see or notice.

For Raven, it might be early, but for life on the

farm, this was considered a sleep-in. Ben's mom, Janette, often reminded her of that. It wasn't easy going back to living with a parent in the house. When in Adelaide, she rented with a friend and was independent. Having his mom around wasn't something she had gotten used to yet, especially when she constantly reminded her that the day had begun hours ago.

Raven checked the internet connection. It was good today. Another thing she'd not thought of was how unreliable the internet connection was out here in the middle of nowhere. Running her own business needed the internet, and she had anticipated that she could work anyway. Not quite.

But today was looking like it would work out. She took a sip of her coffee and then checked her emails, hoping there was some interest from people needing a graphic designer. Setting up her own online graphic design business had been more difficult than she'd thought.

The birds tweeted in the surrounding eucalyptus trees, inspiration took hold, and she put together a series of pre-made logos to upload on her website. Time melted away.

"I asked if you want a cuppa?"

Raven looked up blankly from her screen, her mind pulling ruefully from the creative space she'd been absorbed in.

Janette stood there by the back door, holding open the screen door. "Cuppa?" She was wearing a summer dress—flowy dark green with flowers on it—something typical women her age wore.

"I'm good, thank you," Raven answered. She reminded herself that Janette meant well. The interruption wasn't helpful. Her coffee sat mostly drunk, now cold.

"Did you want some morning tea?"

"I'm good."

"I meant a snack? It's nearly eleven o'clock."

"I'll be fine till lunch. I don't want to put you out." She tried to hide the frustration in her voice from the interruption. Every day was like this. Raven would be absorbed in working on a design on her computer, and low and behold, Janette would have something to say to her. She didn't dare tell Ben this. It was getting harder to put up with, especially as Christmas approached, and Raven wondered what it was going to be like out here. She had considered going back to Adelaide for Christmas with her parents, but a week ago they'd informed her they had booked a mystery deal and were going to have their Christmas dinner somewhere else in Australia. She'd been mortified she had not been considered for Christmas this year, and when she told them as much, they simply responded assuming she'd have it on the farm with Ben and his family. She had, but now that things had changed and her nerves were wearing thin with Janette, the doubt was beginning to grow.

"Just asking." The door slammed closed as Janette went back inside, knocking Raven's thoughts back to reality. She was just sitting on the veranda trying to get some designs completed.

Raven suppressed a sigh as she looked at her computer and tried to focus back on the design she'd been working on. With no new orders this morning, she'd decided to work on pre-made designs to build on her portfolio. Christmas was a week away, and it wasn't likely that she'd get any new clients. At least her existing ones were satisfied with the marketing packages she'd put together for them—Facebook banners, profile images for social media, images sized specifically for Instagram. This was thanks to her friend, Nettie, who was starting up her own vegan chocolate business. Then there was someone Nettie knew, Aaryahi, who needed rebranding for her jewelry-making business. It had been a start, and it meant for a little while she really thought her business in graphic design could actually make it. Now, she wasn't so sure. But with Ben busy with the harvest, and she barely able to see him, usually as he flopped into bed late at night dead tired, Raven really didn't know what else to do with her time. While she wanted to make a living and have her own income, so she could provide for herself here, maybe she had been too rash in deciding it would work for her out here. Was this what it was going to be like for Christmas? Lonely?

Raven sat back in her chair and looked out. Life on the farm was great. Right now, she'd forgotten the earthy animal smell and, instead, breathed in the fresh country air taking in the view of the land. The birds singing were quietening as the day went on and the temperature was rising. Another hot day.

Good thing I don't mind the hot weather.

There was no air conditioning in the old farmhouse, only a standing floor fan and a small rectangular window to open to let in the air. The heat was one thing that wasn't getting to Raven.

A fly buzzed passed her. Flies, on the other hand, were also getting on her nerves. She aimlessly swatted them away, and they continually buzzed around her. She refocused on her computer and the floral design logo she was hoping to finish today.

She'd figured social media would've bridged the gap between life here on the farm and her old life in the city—it kind of did in a way. What Raven hadn't realized was that it wasn't at all a good replacement for the real face-to-face contact she was used to.

Raven had taken to going into the township of Keith frequently to help break up her day and see other people instead of Janette and occasionally Ben. She'd been getting to know Ben's sister, Anne, who was currently working at the local café, Beans. Once or twice she'd gotten a free coffee, which also helped her financially. Raven was all too aware of the cost of petrol from going into town and then for a coffee, just so she could get out of the house and escape for a few hours. Her gut churned tightly at the thought. It was a big indulgent when she wasn't yet able to earn her way here on the farm. But at the same time, it was good for her mental health. She felt the familiar pull to go into Keith now, to take her laptop, sit at Bean at a table out front and watch the little bit of activity happening in the small town while she worked. If she were lucky and it wasn't too busy in the afternoon, maybe Anne could sit and talk to her.

"Here, I bought you some gingerbread biscuits and another coffee for you." Janette placed them in front of her.

"Thanks." Raven pursed her lips tightly together. This was the issue, Janette ignoring her decisions and doing what she thought Raven needed as if she knew better than Raven.

Raven stood up. "I have to go to Keith now, I'll be back for dinner." Then she shut her laptop and left, guilt stabbing at her belly.

"But..."

"I did say no when you asked," said Raven, looking back over her shoulder before she let the screen door slam. In this moment, she had to get out of there.

·   ·   ·

***

B EN GRIPPED the steering wheel of the combine harvester in a relaxed manner as he completed yet another round of the paddock. There was nothing relaxing about how he felt as he kept his eyes on the stalks to ensure they went into the combine and weren't missed.

The air conditioning struggled to keep the cab cool, and Ben could feel sweat from sitting for so long. He knew it was working when he had to get out of the cab, the hot air blasting him as if Mother Nature had decided this area was her oven. If he didn't need to get out, then he would've considered the air conditioning had stopped working hours ago.

There was no way he was going to finish the harvest in the next week, meaning that after Christmas, it was going to be back to work. Today he was reaping the first of the wheat.

The season had been average in this area, and the stalks were shorter than they should've been. Added to this, the crop had been ripe too long and was starting to droop from the strong winds that had ripped through here a week ago. It meant Ben had to set the combine low for the moving knives to catch the stalks of wheat. Any big bumps from rocks or potholes in the paddock could result in the combine hitting the ground and being damaged. He'd already had a minor breakdown early in the season, and he didn't want another to delay the harvest, not when he'd been working such long hours and sacrificing time with Raven to get the crop reaped.

Getting started this morning had been difficult. Raven slept peacefully next to him, and the temptation to lay next to her until she woke and then indulge in some intimacy together had nearly stopped him from getting out of bed. Almost. Years of getting up early meant he kept the discipline. Plus, even if he weren't going to finish harvest before Christmas this year, it still needed to be done. So many things could go wrong before the crop was reaped and delivered to the silos. He didn't want to take any risks, not now that it looked like he was finally going to settle down. He needed an income to support a family, and if things went well, if there was a little extra money, he wanted to give it to Raven to do up parts of the old homestead.

Ben began another round of the paddock. He hoped Raven wasn't feeling rejected. He'd tried to tell her that the harvest was going to be tough, but how did he explain what it was like to a city girl? This was the only life he'd known. He didn't mind not seeing other people during the day and working long hours by himself with his dog, Snipper, by his side. He tried to remember that when thinking of Raven and their future, he needed to come up with some options to help her feel more at home.

It hadn't been the easiest time of year to move to the farm. After the Royal Show in Adelaide, he had to get on the tractor to spray the crops against insect damage, then the weather turned, and the crops ripened enough to begin the harvest. He'd suggested she'd take up tennis, the only summer sport, come to think, the only sport, on offer right now. That hadn't gone down well. Sports weren't her thing. She needed to do something to meet the locals, but with that failure and the business of harvesting, Ben hadn't made any more suggestions.

Raven had given up a lot to live with him on impulse. He didn't want to let her down in any way. It felt like he was doing just that. Plus, he was sensing that maybe things were becoming a little strained between Raven and his mom. That was another issue that would need to be sorted. Where was his mom going to live? He had naïvely hoped they would both get on fabulously. Maybe they would in time? It had barely been three months. It wasn't enough time to cross that option off as a possibility. The bottom line was that Ben wasn't sure what to do. It was great having Raven around, and he didn't want to kick out his mom since she'd aged a lot in the last few years since his father's death. This was her home. He also knew that if things worked between him and Raven, and he was sure it would, then it would be their home. How was he going to find the balance between how things were to how they needed to change?

He finished the round, and without thinking, began another. His saving grace right now was that he had plenty of time to think.

CHAPTER 2

The knots of guilt twisted tight as Raven drove into Keith. It wasn't like her to speak the way she had to Janette. The words had been out, and she'd stormed into the house before her conscience caught up with her. By then, it was too late. That, and the strong desire to get off the farm and go into Keith for some human contact even if she spoke to no one ensured she grabbed her handbag and marched to her car parked in one of the unused old sheds on the property. She had to get out. The view might be inspiring, but the loneliness felt like a cage.

Not use to the unsealed roads and driving the base model white Hyundai Elantra, now covered in a layer of dust, her speed was well under the limit. When going into Keith with Ben or Janette, she would clutch on to the side of the seat not sure she'd get there in one piece based on how fast they drove. Ben, in particular, was a bit of a lead foot behind the wheel. She didn't want to risk her car. If things got really bad, she had been considering selling her car. Or would returning to Adelaide be a better option? She wasn't sure. While she'd first met Ben three years ago, their agreement of a yearly affair at the Royal Show had developed into something more lasting. Right now, it was being tested, which was too much for a new relationship between them. Was the pull of attraction still there between them? She hoped so.

Raven parked her car on the street across from Bean and got out, taking her laptop bag with her. A freak gust of hot wind blasted her, filled with a lot of dust. It felt like the grains were being embedded into her skin. She held her breath until the wind died down, turning her head away to stop from breathing in too much of the dust. Then she glanced right, then left, to make sure there was no traffic, even though she was sure there wasn't going to be. The trucks transporting grain this time of year did seem to rattle along the road faster than they should.

She crossed the old bitumen road, vying her favorite seat out front. She pushed on the heavy wooden door, dark green paint peeling off, and stepped inside. There were a variety of different size tables set up inside, all of them empty. This time of year, Bean did more takeaway meals and coffees, so Anne had told her. A few of the people from town would come in for lunch, but she was an hour too early for that.

"Raven, good to see you today," said Anne as she looked up from polishing a spoon with a tea towel. She smiled broadly as she stood up from the stool behind the counter. She wore denim shorts and a red checkered shirt.

"Usual?"

"Thanks." Raven went to get out her purse.

"Shhh, on the house." Anne winked.

"You sure?" After how rude she'd been to Anne's mom this morning, Raven didn't think she deserved any favors. *Would my business work? It might have more of a chance in Adelaide.* Not for the first time this morning her thoughts turned back to the city life she was used to and comfortable with.

"Yes." She moved her head to the door. "Go sit at your favorite seat, and I'll bring it out to you. Boss is out, so this is the best time to do this. As you can see, it's not a busy time."

"Thank you." Raven was very grateful. Buying a coffee every time she came to town was adding up. There was the local library she could go to, and the more she looked at her bank account, the more she began to think that was going to be the only option, that or not even coming into town. For now, she had to go into town to see that there were other people living on the earth. And today, she was getting a coffee. It was lucky for her that this one was going to be 'on the house.'

Raven went outside, sat at her favorite table—the one second from the end—facing along the main street toward the farm, and got out her laptop. Another good thing coming to Bean was the internet connection was a lot better than on the farm. She set up her laptop and began opening a design to work on while she waited for her coffee. It was hard to concentrate. Her mind was a beehive of thoughts that were going nowhere. Could she live on a farm? Not see Ben as much as she'd want? And then, could she live in the same house as his mom? It had been a little weird at first, then Raven had gotten over that feeling, and now she was just plain frustrated.

At least Anne had the right idea of living in town. She'd managed to scrape together a deposit, bought a small house, and was living there with her boyfriend, Kane, who was the local mechanic.

That's what I need—my own space.

Raven looked around her and realized the irony of the thought. There was more than enough space out here.

Perhaps that was the real issue, she mused.

"Here you go." Anne set a large mug of coffee to the side of Raven's laptop.

"Thanks."

Anne sat on the opposite chair, crossed her tanned

legs, her dirty work boots looking out of place for someone who was a waitress. She held her coffee chest height and looked directly at Raven.

"You work too hard, you know," Anne blurted out.

"I'm starting my own business. I have to," Raven shot back. She didn't mean to be so sharp with her response.

"It's nearly Christmas, give it a break."

"This is a time when I can get ahead."

"Is it working?" Raven rolled her lips together. Anne was touching a raw nerve. "I didn't think so."

"Hey, I hadn't answered."

"You didn't need to. Your silence spoke loudly."

"If I keep at it, I'll get there. I have to keep working." That's the last thing that she wanted to do. What would she do with all the extra time she'd have? It wasn't as if Ben were around. And she was hopeless on the farm. She had no idea what needed to be done, so she couldn't even help out. She did know how to collect the eggs, but then his mom usually had the job done before she remembered to go out herself. She felt useless, like a burden.

"Who knows, you might get a burst of creativity after a break. Christmas is a good time for that. So why don't you shut down your laptop?"

Something cracked inside of Raven, and the words she was too scared to speak tumbled out. "What the hell would I do then? It's not like I have friends to hang with, and I don't know what to do on the farm, so I'm useless there, and well, your mom has everything sorted in the kitchen."

"I'm your friend, so you're wrong there." Her tone was gentle as she spoke.

"That's not what I meant." Raven could feel the emotion boiling inside of her.

Anne's eyes soften. "I'm sure Mom wouldn't mind if you cooked a meal now and then."

"It's her kitchen." Raven realized that even if things did work out with Ben, it would always be Janette's kitchen, her home. Never hers. Her eyes filled with tears, and she blinked quickly willing them to go away and not spill out to show how she was really feeling. She didn't want to offend Anne or her family, but fuck, it was all getting too much, and she was beginning to feel like she was about to spiral out of control.

Anne leaned forward and put her hand on Raven's bare arm. "It is, but she'll let you use it, sometimes, and that's all that matters. She might not let on, but she would also enjoy the night off occasionally. You just need to be prepared for that."

A lump formed in Raven's throat, and she couldn't speak. For the first time, she was beginning to see a different perspective of her situation.

"It's not ideal now, but come the new year when harvest and the Christmas crazy rush is over, why not join a club or two?"

"What, like a craft club, do a bit of bitching and stitching?" Raven hadn't even considered a craft—it wasn't what she did. Sure, she could draw, paint a little. After all, she was a graphic designer, but most of her work was done on the computer. Could she try something new?

Anne laughed, leaning back in her chair. "Or the football club if that's what you want."

"I'll stick with the craft."

"See, not that hard."

"Hmmm, I'm not so sure about that."

"Hey, you've come out here for Ben, and you're the one having to make all the changes, but he'll see it." A shadow crossed Anne's face. "Unless you don't think it's worth it."

The thought of it not being worth it felt suffocating to Raven. She looked away from her to hide her face and the tears threatening to spill. Anne's words were harsh. They hit the nerve and brought all the thoughts she didn't want in her mind to the surface for consideration.

"Anne, does your boss know you're out here?" asked a middle-aged woman as she approached the two women. Raven knew the lady was Anne's boss, and she'd just been busted for not working.

"Gene, don't you go sacking me, now." Anne quickly got up. "I better get back to polishing the silverware." She smiled at Raven, paused, leaned closer, lowing her voice. "You'll work it out."

"Anne, I'm not paying you to be this social," grumbled Gene as she pushed the front door of Bean and stepped inside.

"Coming." She rushed back inside, leaving Raven sitting alone.

Raven wiped the corner of her eyes and turned her computer off. Three months in, and she wasn't about to go back to Adelaide and say this hadn't worked out, but it was getting more and more tempting to do so. There were two loud questions in her head, which she had no clue of the answers.

Is Ben worth it? Are we worth it?

***

RAVEN SLAMMED SHUT HER LAPTOP. Anne was right. A break would be a good idea. She figured the mini-holiday would only be over Christmas and New Years, then she could get back into premade logo designs and do some word-of-mouth advertising on social media to help get her business off the ground.

It was time she faced whatever it was that was scaring her by allowing herself to take a break. She figured the fear was due to two reasons. First, if her business failed, then she'd have no income here, and the thought of what she'd do then was daunting. Second, she didn't want to confront the loneliness she felt away from her friends and family. With the approach of Christmas, she didn't want to face either, but she knew with a twist in her belly that it was time to. Then, there was the real root of her fear. If she had more time to think, she'd drive herself crazy wondering if Ben was ever going to find time for her anytime soon. It worried her that she might crack, throw in the towel, head back to Adelaide, and end up having Christmas all alone this year.

She sipped her coffee while looking down the main street. Cars drove along, some of the drivers waved at her even though she didn't know who they were. Most people seemed to know her—Ben's girlfriend. The times she'd been in Keith having coffee, everyone had been friendly to her as if welcoming her into the community. Coming from the city, she wasn't used to such behavior. There was a lot out here that she wasn't used to. Raven realized she hadn't actually gotten out enough to meet the locals and get to know anyone. Sure, there'd been the handful of occasions when Ben had taken her out on a date to the local pub for a meal, so she'd met a few people then. It had been such a blur, and she'd not considered a pub meal a date, especially when they were interrupted by people the entire time. All she'd focused on was her business and time with Ben.

What sort of club could I join out here?

She wasn't sure that's what she wanted to do, but she did recognize it was another very good suggestion from Anne. Raven wanted to be here for the long term. She wasn't aiming for a short time with Ben—not since they admitted the strong attraction they had for each other, and their fling had developed into a relationship.

Maybe there's an art group? Or drawing or something?

Then she had the crazy idea that if there weren't one, maybe she could start one.

But who would come? I don't know anyone.

Her thoughts were racing, and she forced herself to take a slow, deep breath. First, she needed to find out if there were an art group in town, or what other groups were around that might appeal to her.

She finished her coffee and glanced at her cell to check the time. It was nearly one o'clock. It was also getting a lot warmer outside, even for her. She thought she heard something about a fire ban starting today on the radio that was filtering out from the café. A vague recollection that it could mean Ben might have to come in from the paddocks caused her to want to at least be on the farm if that were the case. But, considering how rude she'd been this morning to Janette, she didn't want to go back to the farm yet. There was no reason to stay here in town. She put her laptop in its carry bag and slung it over her shoulder. As she turned to leave, she noticed a collection of notices stuck to Bean café's glass window. She leaned in and read them.

Raven smiled. There were a few groups advertising meet times for the new year. There were possibilities. She mentally crossed off going along to darts on Tuesday evenings at the pub, though she might give it a go if she got really bored being on the farm. A craft group, Busy Bees, caught her interest. They did a different craft idea each month, and that appealed to her creative mind. It would be good to learn new techniques as well as meeting people. She just hoped there were going to be a few people her age who attended.

Raven took a photo of the printed A4 sign of the upcoming meeting times and activities for the first three months of next year. She also noted that there were a couple of dates with TBA—to be advised—next to them.

Perhaps I could do a painting class or two. The idea sat well in her belly. Raven began to feel her usual confident mojo return. All she needed to do was to turn up with an open mind, and she could do that.

Feeling more relaxed, she decided to go back to the farm. She'd rather try to smooth things over with Janette sooner than later. *If I can.*

Raven wasn't sure about offering to cook a meal or two to help Janette, but she figured it might be a sort of olive branch approach she could do that might work.

What would I cook?

That was if Janette actually would let Raven cook in her kitchen.

I'm not the best cook either.

Raven got in her car and started driving. She figured if she kept it simple, maybe a Waldorf salad with lamb and mint sausages from the local butcher, she could pull off a meal and not make too much of a mess in Janette's kitchen. Determination bubbled inside of her. Anne had somehow said the right things to get her motivated again. Things weren't going to work with Ben if she weren't trying. She just hoped that this was going to be enough.

Raven parked her car back in the shed and waited a moment for the dust to settle before getting out. The cat, Rex, sat on a bale of hay to the side licking his paw as if he'd just had a meal.

She grabbed her laptop bag and purse and then walked to the house. Janette was outside hanging a load of washing. Raven cringed when she saw her knickers hanging on the line.

"You didn't have to do my washing, Janette," Raven tried to keep her voice polite. She didn't like the idea that Janette had been in her room. Raven liked to keep things neat, so all her dirty washing had been put in a wash basket she kept in the corner of the room she and Ben shared, but still, she did like her privacy. She and Ben were always discreet, considering how hot things had been between them when they met up at the show which hadn't always been easy.

"It's no trouble at all." Janette smiled at her from behind a towel. "It's good drying weather. These will all be inside, ironed, and dried before dark."

"But I'm making more work for you," said Raven trying to be diplomatic in her approach with Janette. Not like this morning.

"Pfft. You're no work at all." Janette stepped to the side and took another damp towel from the basket and pegged it to the clothesline that stood to the side of the open backyard. "You've got your business work to do, so I thought if I did your washing, then you'd get more done."

Raven's heart squeezed with guilt. "Thank you." She resisted the urge to go inside and get working on designs right there and then. "I need to earn my keep here, so I thought that maybe I could do some of the cooking... maybe make the evening meal once or twice a week?"

"Don't be silly. You don't need to make a meal to earn your keep around here. You've made my Ben a happy man. That's all I want."

Raven felt her cheeks flush with heat. *Have we been discrete enough?* At least they were never caught 'in the act' by Janette.

"I mean he's happier generally having you in his life. When he asked if you could move in, I wasn't so sure. I hadn't even met you. But then I saw how his face lit up when he mentioned you, I had to say yes."

Raven hadn't known Ben had asked his mom if she could move in. Things had happened so quickly, she'd just assumed Ben had told her instead of asking for permission. It warmed her heart to think he'd respected his mom like that.

"I need to do some of the workload around here. Besides, I'm going to have a break from my designing in the lead-up to Christmas, and who knows when I'll see Ben again, he's so busy with the harvest." The words flooded out as if knowing that Janette had agreed she could live here broke some of the tension between them.

"Good idea you're taking a break. You work so hard."

"I want this business to succeed, a lot is riding on it." She realized that she'd thought if it didn't work, then maybe things wouldn't work out with Ben either. Fear had a way of being so irrational.

"Less than you know. Ben will take very good care of you, always."

Raven wasn't sure what to say to that. Her feelings were too mixed. Was this the life for her? Could she ever fit in?

"Have you been out on the harvester yet?" asked Janette.

"No."

"You should ask Ben to take you. Learning how to drive it will help to pass the time."

Raven gleaned at what Janette was doing. It was a good idea. It was long overdue that she was more involved on the farm. So far, there just hadn't been any time to teach her. "I'll do that when I see him next. On one condition."

Janette raised an eyebrow. "What's that?"

"That I cook one meal a week for us all."

Janette sighed as if she were grappling with her inner fears. "Fine."

Raven smiled. "I'll cook Sunday night, then." What she wasn't sure of was would it only be for her and Janette, or would Ben be there too?

CHAPTER 3

Ben stopped the combine alongside the truck, lining it up carefully. He pulled a lever, and the auger swung out from the combine, stopping just where he'd planned over the bin of the truck. He pressed another lever, and grain started spilling out into the truck.

It was getting on in the day, but there was still plenty of daylight hours left, which he hoped he could take full advantage of.

His cell buzzed. He glanced at the screen. The message was from his mate, Jason.

Fuck it.

Ben thought to himself. This wasn't at all what he needed to be reminded of. Sure, there was no hard and fast rule if he kept harvesting in this extreme heat. But if there were a spark from his combine, it would start a fire, and there were unreaped paddocks of his neighbors that could end up burning, not just his. He didn't want to be the idiot to cause a fire like that.

Just stopping now.

Fuck.

Ben breathed out with frustration as the last of the grain transferred from the combine to the truck. This was it for the day. He was done working out here.

He glanced at the weather outlook on his cell. There should be a slight cooling change tonight, so he could get back out here tomorrow. If he were lucky, the weather might be just a few degrees cooler by then and the fire ban lifted. He needed to keep working these long hours if he wanted to get the harvest finished and get the much-needed income.

Ben let the engine of the combine idle for a little while, so it would cool, before turning it off. His mind shifted through the very long list of jobs that needed to be done on the farm, which weren't getting done while he had the harvest to focus on. There was the section of fence that needed fixing in the north paddock. Then, he needed to get some more feed for the alpacas. The machinery could do with a bit of oiling. If the truck was full, then he could take the load to the silos, but it wasn't.

If only I could've got a few more rounds done, Ben thought wistfully. *Then the truck would've been full, and at least I would've been able to deliver the load.*

That would also mean he was one step closer to being paid for the grain, which could still take months before that would happen. There was no point agonizing over what could've been, there was so much he could do right now.

Then there was also the Christmas shopping he should go and do. Hell, he hated going into the shops. But this year, he needed to get something for Raven. It was her first Christmas with him and his family on the farm. He wanted to get her something special because, well, because he loved her. And she'd given up so much to come and live with him, to give them a chance of having a relationship and a future together. With the farm, there was no way he could've ever moved to the city. This was the way it had to be. So far, he was thinking things were working out very well between them.

Maybe it's not so bad having to stop now, he mused,

recognizing the very big silver lining to this cloud of having to stop here. If he went back to the farm now, there was a good amount of time he could spend with Raven, and well, he knew exactly how that was going to go. He couldn't wait to get her naked and familiarize himself with her curvy body, but another, more sobering thought stopped this fantasy.

Ben didn't want to think how bad he would look if he didn't manage to get Raven a Christmas gift, even if it were hard with the long hours since the shops were usually closed when he finished for the day.

The shops it is, he decided as he turned off the engine. If he were quick enough, then he could go back to the farm and spend some time with Raven. She'd been so patient with him working such long hours at this time of year, especially since she had no idea of what farm life was like.

Ben jumped out and strode over to the ute. While he was in Keith, he'd pick up the feed he needed. This was working out better than he thought it would. Though the problem was, he had absolutely no idea what to get Raven. He'd never been very good at buying gifts. He wanted to give her something meaningful as this was a big deal having their first Christmas together, and he didn't want to mess it up.

It was all he could think about during the twenty-minute drive into Keith. What the hell was he going to buy Raven? He couldn't even think what he'd get his mom or Anne. They were used to him being late with his gifts, or even opting for gift cards, over Christmas. He knew that Raven wouldn't be satisfied with that.

Not this year. Perhaps not any year.

Ben slowed down as he approached the outskirts of Keith. Houses now lined either side of the road instead of the open spaces of land. He was already starting to feel penned in, and he hadn't got to the center of town yet.

With no idea of what sort of gift to buy Raven, Ben decided to get the feed loaded up for the alpacas first. He drove to the agricultural store in town, parked out the back, and then strode inside. It was so easy this time of year to forget it was Christmas on account of the harvest and the long hours he had to work.

Out of the corner of his eye, he saw women's work boots. An idea sparked in his head.

I can't get that for Raven. Or can I?

He went over to the range of work boots. They were what she needed when out on the farm. He'd been meaning to invite her to come with him on the harvester, but she'd always seemed too busy on her computer. He didn't want to interrupt the work she was doing for her graphic design business.

He picked up a pair. In a way, he thought it might be safer to stick to chocolates and maybe a necklace, but the work boots felt right to give her. Things had been slow, it had been a fling, but then Raven moving in, things had progressed very quickly. It was time to tread a little water and just see how things were going to go. Even though Ben was certain it was going well between them.

"Can I help you, Ben?" asked John, one of the owners of the agricultural store.

"I'll take these." Ben had to guess at the size of Raven's feet.

"You sure on the size?"

"You'll do an exchange if I'm wrong?" Ben handed the box to John.

"For you. Now, do you want it gift wrapped?"

Ben raised his eyebrow. "You do gift wrapping now, do you?"

John chuckled, "No, but these are a gift for your new girl, so things are getting serious?"

Were they? Raven had moved in with him, and hell, that was very serious.

"I'll grab a box of chocolates."

"We don't have chocolates."

"I'm sure they'd be a best seller with the guys coming in here needing to smooth things over with their missus."

"I think you might be on to something."

"I'll get the feed, too, while I'm here."

"Okay, I'll get Dave to help me load them up on your ute. Two dozen?"

"Yep, that'll get us into the new year until you open up again."

"Right-o. Give me a minute to gift wrap this, and I'll put it all on your account."

Ben grinned at John's sense of humor. It would certainly be helpful if he could gift wrap the boots. A glance at his cell and all Ben wanted to do now was to get home and have a bit of time with Raven. Wrapping paper and card could wait. At least he managed to get a gift. With any luck, Raven would like it.

***

RAVEN LEANED on the old wooden railing and looked out into the paddock of alpacas. There were a few blades of green grass, but mainly it was brown, burned by the summer sun, even though it was only December and summer was only beginning. She shaded her eyes with her hand, wishing she'd grabbed her sunglasses on the way out of the house. This was a view she could look at for hours.

The male alpha stood nearly as tall as his mother, Evie, head down nibbling at the hay Ben had spread around early this morning. He was a beautiful tan color, big eyes, and long ears. Ben thought he would keep him for breeding instead of selling him, much to Raven's delight. There was a special connection she had for Evie after seeing her give birth at the Royal Show only a few months ago. It was also the start of the relationship with Ben being more than a yearly fling. Raven didn't think she could bear to see the young stud boy sold. She was even looking forward to when Evie would be a mother again next year. Raven surprised herself with her thoughts.

Wow, I have learned things about the farm. The emotion of feeling lonely bubbled under the surface, but she ignored it. That was the biggest issue she had here, and it could be enough to break the connection with Ben. She still had to wait for the group meetings to start up again after the festive holidays, and who knew how well her cooking for Janette would really go. She hoped these changes were going to be enough to stave off the feeling of isolation here.

Raven was nervous about cooking for Janette and Ben. That was if Ben even made it to the dinner table Sunday night. In all likelihood, he would be on the harvester. She had no idea what to cook. Her best dish was a honey-soy stir fry, but somehow, she didn't think that was quite what Janette was used to.

Could I do meat and three vegetables?

That simple dish didn't inspire her. Then there was an Indian lamb korma curry she could cook, but again, would that be something Janette or even Ben would enjoy? Cooking wasn't her strong point—

Janette had years of experience and was a very good cook.

Maybe I should've just offered to always be on clean up, she mused as Evie lifted her head and looked at her, chewing a mouthful of hay before putting her head back down, her lips moving to nibble at more. A few of the alpacas had settled in the shade of the trees and had nestled down resting the afternoon away.

The heat from the sun radiated, and sweat began to bead on her forehead, but Raven didn't mind so much. The warmth of the day seemed to give her a bit of comfort that she needed right now. That, and watching Evie in the paddock with the other alpacas.

Feeling that things had somewhat been smoothed over with Janette, Raven had come out to clear her head in the fresh air—air that smelled of an animal earthiness. A gentle breeze moved the excess material of her loose pants. She remembered how alone she was out here and how she was disconnected with her old life and not yet connected with this new life. Another warm tickle from the wind moved over her body. A swim would be good right about now. The beach was too far away to bother driving to, and there was no pool on the farm. When she'd asked Ben what he'd done as a kid to cool down, he'd muttered something about running through the garden sprinklers. Right now, she considered that could be an option if it meant it helped her to cool down.

As much as she didn't mind the extremely hot weather, right now, it was starting to get a little uncomfortable, so she considered going back into the house. But there was no air conditioning, and in an attempt to keep it cool, Janette had closed all the windows and shut the blinds and curtains to keep it dark. It helped to keep the temperature down inside, but it also made Raven feel a little claustrophobic.

It was too early to collect the afternoon eggs from the dozen or so chooks they had on the farm, so she'd decided to visit Evie. A few of the galahs squawked in the surrounding trees, then settled—it was too hot for them to cause a ruckus.

Raven could hear the chooks clucking. A few had ventured near her, scratching at the ground and pecking as if the heat was no problem for them. Even Rex, the cat, hadn't come down with her like he often did. She was beginning to think that maybe an afternoon rest would be a good way to pass the last of the hot afternoon before it hopefully started to cool down again. Janette had mentioned that there should be a bit of a cooling change. Raven hoped so.

The sound of a vehicle engine rattling down the driveway caused Raven to look behind her, wondering who would be visiting. She still wasn't used to how neighbors dropped in at random times with no warning.

It was Ben's ute, and it was loaded high with bags of

alpaca feed. She frowned. Why had he gone into town? And why wasn't he on the harvester?

A knot formed in her gut, and a shiver went down her spine. Had something gone wrong?

She exhaled slowly, realizing how quickly she was jumping to conclusions.

Was this what it was like to be a farmer's wife? she suddenly thought. Raven didn't much like how she was feeling right now, simply seeing Ben drive here with his ute, knowing that he should be out harvesting the crop.

CHAPTER 4

Ben smiled to himself as he saw Raven standing by the alpacas. She wore her city clothes—long loose pants and tight top—instead of the usual jeans and shirt that no matter the weather the locals wore. Her style looked a little out of place, but also at the same time, it was perfect, a breath of fresh air. A change. Something new and fun, but also strong, reliable, and sassy. That's what drew him to her. He enjoyed driving into his home and seeing her. His pulse increased, and his body started to respond with the primal desires he'd been denying.

He glanced at the package on the passenger seat next to him. Would she like it? Would this be the gift to mark their first Christmas together?

Ben drove the ute to the shed where he stored the alpaca feed and parked the ute. He needed to unload it now, but there was something way more important he needed to do. As he got out, Snipper came up to him, excited that he was home. The dog jumped up and down, wagging his tail madly.

"Hey, boy." Ben paused to give Snipper a scratch behind his ears before making his way down to the alpacas to Raven.

She turned and smiled as he walked up to her. His heart skipped so many beats he was sure it was out of control from just seeing her, standing relaxed watching the alpacas as if it were the most natural thing for her to do, despite being a city girl.

"Keeping an eye on them for me?" he asked, wrapping his arms around her narrow waist and pulling her to him. He could feel her easing into his embrace as if their souls were melding with each other.

"Well, I don't really know what to keep an eye on."

"You'd surprise yourself. Sometimes you just know when something is wrong." He nuzzled into her neck. She smelled divine—a mix of floral perfume with her pheromones. Desire flooded his body.

She looked up at him. A serious expression took hold over her face, cute lines formed on her forehead and in the corners of her eyes. He didn't let her talk. Instead, he planted his lips on hers. Her salty flavor exploded in his mouth, and he gently danced his tongue over hers, savoring. It had been too long. He moved his hands over her backside, grabbing them and squeezing playfully, enjoying hearing her gasp from his touch.

She gently pulled away from the kiss, nestling her back into his chest and resting her head so that he could nuzzle the side of her neck.

It might have been a while since they had their sexy fun time, but the way he felt with Raven in his arms, was natural. She wrapped her arms over his.

"Why aren't you out on the tractor?" she asked. She leaned into his body, and he easily took her weight.

"Harvester, you mean?"

"Same thing."

He chuckled. "Not even close."

Ben held her to him tighter, enjoying feeling all of her body against his, pushing his hardness into her, moving his hips in a subtle grinding fashion. She sighed with pleasure, and he felt her body relax further. Pleasure shot through his body, and he fought the temptation to rush things.

He moved his hands over her belly, then down the front of her hips, and over the top of her thighs. Fuck, she felt good to touch like this. He wanted more, to feel all of her. He pressed his hands firmly into her body, moving them back up over her curves. Her body arched into him. His hands cupped around her breasts, and he massaged his fingers into her soft flesh, feeling her nipples harden through the material.

Forcing himself to take his time, he released his

grip on her breasts, slipping his hands once more down her body. His fingers found the top of the waistband of her pants, and he pushed under the material. Her hips moved forward as if guiding him where to go. He knew exactly where to touch her. He brushed a hand over the lacy material of her panties in a teasing motion. She reached up, wrapping her hands behind his head. He kissed the side of her neck, running his tongue along her salty skin to the base of her collarbone.

His fingers found the top of her panties, dove under the material, and moved through her pubes to her slit. She moaned as he moved his hand further between her legs, enjoying the slipperiness of her juices that had pooled quickly. He rested one hand low on her abdomen as the other worked between her intimate folds. Her hips rocked to increase the pressure of his touch, and the sounds of pleasure escaping her lips encouraged him to keep drawing the pleasure from her body.

He moved his thumb to the top of her slit, finding the nub of nerves to massage, and systematically increased the pressure, taking her to a peak. Her orgasm blossomed, bursting through her body in a sweet series of convulsions in time with her gasps.

"Felt good, hey," he whispered into her ear. She sighed with pleasure, eyes closed, her facial expression clear she'd enjoyed every second.

Slowly, he removed his hand. She sighed with a hint of disappointment.

"It's not over yet."

Fuck, he wanted to be inside of her.

He spun her around to face him. She looked up at him, a hint of surprise in her eyes. It only made him want her more.

"What if someone sees us?"

"Who?" He raised his eyebrow. They were far enough away from the house that they wouldn't be seen. The alpacas didn't care about them. All that mattered was them, and he planned to take full advantage of this time together.

CHAPTER 5

Raven blushed as she dressed. "I can't believe we just did that."

Ben laughed. "Yes, you can." He pulled up his jeans. "We used to do this only once a year, or have you forgotten?"

"I haven't forgotten." Though it had felt like a longer wait than a year, which was stupid because, of course, it hadn't been. "It's just good to..." She felt the heat intensify on her cheeks.

"What, fuck me in nature?"

She playfully slapped him on the arm and laughed. "No. Yes." She rolled her eyes.

"You're confusing a man here." He winked at her.

Raven paused, lowered her voice. "I've missed this."

"Raven, I'm sorry." He embraced her. Warmth wrapped around her, and she rested her head on his chest, breathing in his masculine scent, hinted with dust. She like this new smell of his.

"I shouldn't have said anything." This wasn't the time to bring in how lonely she feels, not when she had a plan to get more involved, but somehow, the words had slipped out.

"I want to say that it's not always going to be like this, but it will every year at this time. Then there's the seeding time before winter." He looked into her eyes. She felt herself go weak in the knees. There was no doubt there was a deep attraction between them. He brushed a loose piece of hair back behind her ear.

"But you need to know I'm still here, working hard for a future for us."

When he spoke 'us,' a shiver went through her body. She believed him.

"I know." She did know this, and it helped to keep the loneliness she'd been feeling at bay.

"You've given up so much. I want you to know there are no words to express how grateful I am that you're willing to take a chance on me."

"On us," she corrected.

He smiled, his eyes lighting up. "On us." He kissed her softly.

"There are always things to be doing on the farm, but I'll make time for you when I can, always."

"I should hope so." She winked at him.

He cupped his hands around her jawline, stared deeply into her eyes. "I know so."

Her skin prickled. How she hoped that his words would keep the feeling of isolation away. She kissed him.

"Now, I'm sorry, but – "

"Let me guess, you got a job to do."

"Yes."

"Can I help?"

She couldn't help smiling at the look of surprise on his face.

Ben took Raven's arm and inspected it.

"What are you doing?" she asked.

"Checking to see if you have the muscle power for the job that needs to be done."

Raven's jaw dropped, then she realized he was teasing her. She punched him in the top of his arm as hard as she could.

"Aw." He rubbed his arm.

"So, do you think I'd be strong enough?"

He chuckled. "I do."

"Then lead the way."

"I need to unload the feed for the alpacas, but the bags might be a bit heavy for you."

"I'll try." Raven meant it too. She really wanted to give life on the farm with Ben a go.

"I think you're more of a country girl than you realize." He put his arm over her shoulder and guided her toward the shed.

"Well, with that in mind, do you think I could join you on the harvester?" There, she'd implemented part of the plan. For some reason, her pulse raced. Would he really want her around, especially when she had no idea how to help or even if she could?

"I'd love you to join me but only because you used the correct term."

She rolled her eyes. "You're a hard person to impress sometimes."

He leaned in closer to her, his breath hot on her neck. "You looked pretty impressed with me a few minutes ago."

She blushed, looked at him with her cheeky expression. "As did you with me."

He laughed. "Come on, let's get this job done, and maybe we could get some more time to *impress* each other."

"Sounds like a very good plan to me."

Her stomach fluttered with excitement. This was going to be much better than working on her graphics or doing nothing on the farm. She had wanted an adventure by moving here, and it was long overdue to step things up to the next level.

***

.   .   .

BEN SLID the last bag of feed to the end of the tray on his ute. He jumped down. "Ready?"

"Yes." Raven grabbed the two ends of the bag, he the other, and together they lifted the heavy bag. "I've never been to a gym before, but this is got to be a better workout."

He laughed. "I've never been either, so I wouldn't know."

"Tell me, then, is this how you get your arm muscles so toned? Moving two dozen bags of feed that weigh a bloody ton."

"You telling me I've got arm muscles?"

"You're getting too carried away." She rolled her eyes.

Ben could've done this job by himself, taking less time, but it had been much more enjoyable with Raven helping him. It was a real treat to have someone not to just help him but also to talk to.

Her willingness to get hands-on and not shy away from hard work caused his attraction to her strengthen even more. Like right now. She looked sexy, in her loose pants, low-cut top, and sweat shining on her fore-head. Her top was dusty, and there was dirt smeared on her arms. She kept helping him without complaint, or any concern about her clothes, or even if she might break a nail. Raven was a hell of a find in his life those three years ago, and he was feeling lucky. Hell, he'd just got lucky with her, thanks to the hot weather. Watching her work alongside him, he was starting to feel his desires return. They had a bit of time to make up in terms of sexy fun. Ben quite liked the idea that he might get lucky again today. There were half a dozen jobs he should do, but with Raven looking desirable, all he wanted was to be with her.

Ben kept shuffling backward slowly, checking to see if they were nearly at the other bags and keeping an eye on how well Raven was doing. This was the last bag, and they'd done this twenty-three times already.

He could see Raven straining and trying to keep hold of the bag. Her arm muscles were taut, knuckles white as she kept the grip on the bag as he shuffled backward into the shed to the pile of bags they had just unloaded.

"You okay?" he asked, not for the first time. He had a feeling she wasn't about to admit if she weren't or if she needed to stop for a break. He wasn't sure how she was managing to keep going like she was. For him, it was different—he was used to this sort of work. She wasn't.

Raven clenched her jaw together, determination spread across her face and nodded.

He glanced behind him and was relieved to see they were almost at the stack of feed.

"Drop it here, on top."

He saw her about to lose her hold and quickly changed his grip to take the bag.

"Fuck," she cursed as he took the bag, swinging it easily on top of the pile.

"Did you hurt yourself?"

She shook her head. "I just was so close to getting through without dropping a bag. I wanted to show you that I could do the farm work with you."

Ben's heart melted hearing her words. He strode over, scooped her up into his arms, lifting her off the ground. A surprised squeal came from her as he spun her around before lowering her back down.

"I'm so impressed with you." He gazed into her eyes. "You worked so hard."

"Really?"

"Absolutely."

"How impressed are you?" She raised an eyebrow suggestively.

He grinned. "This impressed." He pressed his lips on hers, slowly parting them with his. She leaned into him, returning the kiss, and he felt the connection between them intensify.

"I don't think you're really showing me how impressed you are." Her eyes sparkled with cheekiness.

He blew softly on her neck, nibbled at her skin playfully, enjoying seeing her shiver with pleasure.

"Better?"

"Getting there. My arms are a bit sore. Come to think of it, I'm sore all over." She pushed her body into his.

"Are you suggesting something in particular?" He knew damn well she was angling for a massage.

"Whatever you think would show me properly how impressed you are with my work ethic."

He grinned, reached down, and grabbed her hand. "We better go inside then."

"And why's that?" She let him lead her back toward the house.

"Follow me, and you might well find out."

"Sounds like an offer too good to refuse."

"You better believe it." He glanced at the shed and noticed his mom's car wasn't there. "And things have just gotten even better for us."

"How?" She frowned.

"Mom's car isn't in the shed, so the house is ours."

Raven squealed playfully, shook her hand free from his and started running toward the house. She looked back over her shoulder. "Hurry up, then."

Ben laughed. He didn't need to be told twice. He rushed to catch up with Raven. He might not be about to be harvesting because of the weather, but this was the perfect way to spend a hot afternoon.

***

· · ·

"I NEED A SHOWER FIRST," said Raven as she opened the screen door. She hated to think how badly she must smell right now, and her clothes felt like they were clinging to her body.

"You smell fine to me." Ben quickly put toe to heel on one boot and pulled it off, then did the other.

Raven wondered if she should've done that to her slip-on shoes. She lifted each foot to look at the sole. Fortunately, they were clean, just a bit dusty which was nothing unusual for around here. At least there was no animal shit—she was getting better at keeping an eye on where she was walking when out on the farm. The last thing she wanted to be doing was cleaning shit off her shoes.

I should get some work boots.

"Is your nose blocked or something? I'm pretty sure I stink." She could feel her shirt sticking to her back from the sweat.

"You're fine." He padded over to her, wrapped his arms around her, and breathed in deeply as if to prove it.

Raven laughed, trying to push out of the embrace. "Maybe you should have a shower," she teased.

"Hey, I don't smell. I'm a working man." He grinned at her, keeping his arms around her.

"Well, working man, what about a shower?" Raven

managed to get out of his grip, then slipped inside, and he followed trying to grab her. She laughed and started to move toward the hallway to the room they shared.

"Where you going?" Ben asked as he moved toward the right to the bathroom. "I thought you wanted a shower?"

"Yeah, but I need to get fresh clothes," she called out to him. He had disappeared.

"Why? There's just us here."

His cheeky tone fueled her curiosity, and she walked back and poked her head into the lean-to of the house where the laundry and bathroom were.

She wolf-whistled, leaned against the door frame, and took in the sight.

Ben stood there, his back to her and butt-naked, putting his clothes straight into the washing machine.

"Stop staring," he said with a wink as he glanced over his shoulder at her.

"I can't. This isn't a sight I normally see," answered Raven. His toned muscles from the physical work on the farm were a delight to see. He had tan lines on his arms from where he'd rolled up his shirt when working, but overall, his skin was a lovely olive tone.

"You're not going to join me for a shower?" he asked as he put in some soap powder and then set the dials for the washing cycle. "Or you're going in fully clothed?"

Instead of answering him, Raven walked up to Ben

and embraced him from behind. The heat in his body seeped into hers, sending her need skyrocketing.

"Oh, hello." He still messed around with the dials. The beeping a distraction as he flicked between the programs. "I can never work this thing."

"So, this is all show for me, is it?"

"Damn right it is."

She giggled, slowly slipped her hand over the front of his hip and over his cock. She took him in her hand, moving back and forth along his length, enjoying how it was hardening. Liquid oozed from its tip, and he groaned softly. She rocked her hips into him as she played her fingers around his tip, pulling the foreskin back and forth. He felt great in her hand. Despite what she'd told him, he smelled fine. She rested her head onto his back, teasing his body toward its peak.

"You're meant to be showing me how impressed you are," she murmured.

"That's right." He spun her around and kissed her as his hands went down to her pants. He broke the kiss and pulled them down along with her panties, kneeling in front of her. She stepped easily from them as she pulled her T-shirt up over her head, letting it float to the ground.

She looked down at him kneeling in front of her. He glanced up, his eyes full of desire. His hands moved up her legs and rested on her hips. Leaning forward, he pressed his mouth onto her mound, kissing hard into her. Her hips naturally rocked forward with the need for more. His tongue flicked down her slit, and she groaned. Her mind spun with the building pleasure. She let her hands fall on his head, her fingers tangling in his hair. He sucked hard into her intimate skin, teasing the pleasure from her body. She closed her eyes, giving over to the sensations he evoked. His tongue danced over the top of her slit playing with the sensitive nerves, pushing her close to her own peak. Her breath quickened, and she tried to hold out, but her body filled quickly with ecstasy, the tension breaking into a delightful orgasm that sent wave after wave of bliss.

She sighed heavily with the last of the convulsions of the orgasm rattling through her. He kissed her mound softly, aware of how much more sensitive she was now.

"Does that tell you enough about how impressed I am?" He looked up at her.

She nodded, smiling, trying to catch her breath as her mind spun with the desire he'd teased from her.

"Good because I'm not finished."

He stood up, running his hands up her body, feeling her curves. He unclipped her bra, moved it away, and then pulled her into his body, her breasts crushing pleasantly into his chest. With the feel of his skin on hers, a fresh wave of desire took hold of her.

"I'm so glad I impressed you," she mumbled, her mind blurring with the desire burning through her.

"Me, too."

He picked her up, turned around, and set her on the washing machine. Automatically, she spread her legs, and he stepped between them, his cock pressing into her lower abdomen. Her muscles contracted, eager to have him inside of her and something to clench onto.

She looked quizzically at him. "Shouldn't it be on, you know, so it's vibrating?"

"I'll have you vibrating soon enough." He winked at her, pulling her hips forward.

She felt his cock positioned at her opening, sitting in the fresh wave of her hot juices.

"Is that right..." She ended the sentence in a gasp of pleasure as he thrust himself into her. "Oh."

He drew out slowly, her muscles going wild with contractions trying to hold on to his cock and keep it inside of her. Then he plunged deep inside of her.

She gasped sharply, a flood of pleasure thundering through her.

Raven leaned back and put her hands on either side of the washing machine to keep her balance. All she could do right now was hold on, which included Ben too. Her legs wrapped around his waist, securing them together as their bodies moved in a quickening rhythm.

"Oh…" She couldn't help the noises escaping from her mouth as he moved in and out of her. Her body tingled as if the pleasure vibrating through her was taking hold and lifting her to her peak. Her breath came quick and shallow. She felt his body tighten. He groaned, and his movements became more deliberate, which spiked the heat in her body as he pounded her, pushing her with him toward their peak. Her body convulsed with the orgasm, and he moved in and out once more, then reached his orgasm as hers took hold. She called out his name, her mind spun with the dizzying vibrations he had indeed coaxed from her.

"Hmmm." He pulled her into his arms and nuzzled their noses together.

Raven wrapped her arms around his neck and kissed him. "Now I really do know that you're impressed with me, and you know you didn't need the washing machine on."

"I told you." He kissed her.

"And, um, you don't smell either." She winked at him.

"You're getting cheekier the longer you stay here."

She smiled at him. "I'm learning from you."

"Don't go blaming me." He grinned at her, reached out and moved his hands lovingly through her long hair.

She chuckled. "How about that shower and massage?"

"You've not had enough?" His eyes widened in surprise.

"Oh, you've satisfied me very well. I just want to keep you to myself for a little longer."

"Well, in that case." He lifted her from the top of the washing machine. "Shower, it is."

The sound of a car door slamming caused them both to freeze.

"Did you hear that?" whispered Raven.

"Shit, yes."

"Who do you think it is?" Raven couldn't think properly, not after the wonderful session they'd just had.

He cleared his throat. He didn't need to say because Raven's mind finally grounded, and she realized who it was likely to be.

"Quick," he said, dragging her toward the hallway.

"My clothes…"

"Don't worry about that," he said. He tried to push her toward the hallway.

Raven couldn't help it, she had to look. She glanced at the back door and saw his mom.

Shit. His mom was too close.

Raven turned and ran with Ben, just as the screen door opened.

"Oh." A surprised sound filtered from behind them. Raven didn't dare look. The heat from sex had turned to a chilling cold as she ran up to their bedroom. They got inside and closed the door.

Ben panted leaning back on the bedroom door. "That was too close."

"I'm so embarrassed." Raven shook her head. How was she going to face Janette? "I'll have to live in here forever now."

"No, don't worry about it."

"I don't see how you can be so relaxed about it."

"I'm not, but Mom, well, she'll be as embarrassed as us, so she won't mention it. Just go on as normal."

Raven swallowed hard. "Go on as normal? That's your solution?"

"You got a better one?"

Raven shook her head.

"Just think it could've been worse."

Raven raised an eyebrow at Ben. This was how he was thinking? This was bloody bad enough. Then she saw the glint in his eyes. She couldn't help it. She giggled softly, and so did Ben.

"Best to laugh it off, hey," whispered Ben.

"Only thing to do." She shook her head and went up to Ben and hugged him.

"Come on, best get dressed and face the music."

"Now?" Raven stopped laughing, and the embarrassment returned.

"Consider it like removing a Band-Aid."

Raven rolled her eyes. "Why not." She sure as hell didn't have any better suggestions.

Wishing she'd at least got a shower, she found clean underwear and a summer dress to wear while Ben pulled on clean jeans and an old polo T-shirt with Wrangler embroidered on it.

Taking a deep breath, Ben put his hand on the door. "Ready?"

"No." Raven looked at him wide-eyed. She couldn't believe that she was about to do this.

Ben ignored her, opened the door, and strode out. Raven followed him reluctantly down the short hallway. She could hear his mom in the kitchen.

Ben walked into the kitchen. "Hi, Mom," he said casually.

Raven couldn't believe this was what they were doing. His mom was at the kitchen sink with her back to them. She plonked herself on a chair before her legs gave way on her. So far, at least, his mom hadn't said anything.

"Cuppa?" she asked. Her back still to them.

"That would be great, thanks," said Raven. She had to force herself to speak. All she wanted to do was to run out back to the privacy of the bedroom.

"Good to see you two dressed now," she said as she turned around, her face a stoneless expression.

"Sorry," whispered Raven as a fresh wave of embarrassment washed over her.

"Won't happen again," said Ben. Raven nodded. It wouldn't happen again. Ever. She took a deep breath. This was more complicated than she thought it would be living on the farm with Ben. The doubt slowly began to flutter in her belly again. Could this place ever be just hers and Ben's? That would be the normal thing to expect as a new couple. But things on the farm were far from the normal she was used to. She looked at Ben. He smiled encouragingly at her as if they hadn't nearly been caught in the act. She was attracted to him. She felt the connection there between them which was more than the fling that had started their yearly meet-ups.

Janette put a cup of tea in front of her with a thud. The liquid nearly splashed out, and Raven jumped. She looked up to see a grumpy look on Janette's face. Would living with Ben's mom be the deal-breaker? Be the thing that stopped them from having a future together?

Have we moved forward too quickly? She shivered. She put her hands around the cup of tea, the warmth offering no comfort. One thing was certain—Raven was going to have to work harder in building a rela-tionship with his mom. That's if she wanted to stay here on the farm.

CHAPTER 6

Saturday, December 21st

"You sure there's enough room for me here?" She turned to the left, found it just as uncomfortable and moved back to the right. It was a very tight squeeze in this cab for two adults, even if they were in love with each other.

"Yeah, heaps of room." He didn't even look at her as he concentrated on the controls to his right, moving levers. He sat on the only chair in the cab which, of course, made sense since he was the one driving.

"You'd think they'd design the layout so that there would be an extra chair in this thing."

"I rarely get visitors here with me."

"I can see why," she said sarcastically.

He chuckled to himself. "It's a one-man job harvesting with a machine like this."

"I thought you wanted me here?"

"Of course, I want you here." He reached over and squeezed her arm. The brief touch of his skin on her arm reassured her. Ben returned his attention to getting started. The combine's engine roared into life.

Raven smiled, feeling the power of the machine vibrating around her. It was exciting and a bit scary both at the same time. She had no idea what Ben was doing as he checked through a series of switches. Come to think of it, she had no clue as to what was going to happen next. A shiver of nerves moved in her belly, and she held on to the back of the chair to steady herself. She'd never been inside heavy machinery like this before. This was so removed from her life in the city that it made her head spin. Raven wriggled again in hopes she might find a better position but with no luck. It wasn't much fun sitting on the arm of the chair.

"Keep still."

Raven froze. "Sorry."

She wasn't sure why she needed to be still, but there was a look of concentration on Ben's face, and she didn't want to be the one to break it with questions. Right now, she was in a situation where she would do as she was told.

The air conditioning blew out dusty air, and she was beginning to find the space too confined. The radio crackled, the reception lost. Raven reached up and tried to re-tune it, but when that didn't work, she turned it off.

What the hell was I thinking? She glanced at Ben, who looked back at her. His grin brightened up his eyes which lightened the dark shadows from being so tired. Not that she would've known, after their session outside yesterday, she was rewarded with another longer one inside when they found out they had the house to themselves. It was just unfortunate Janette had come home earlier than she and Ben had anticipated.

To have had the time to reconnect with Ben was just what she needed. She hoped that spending this time on the farm with him now, helping him, would help give her more of an idea of what life was going to be like with him.

So far, she wasn't sure it was helping. This morning had been hard. Instead of Ben slipping out of bed without waking her, he'd reached for her, rolling over to snuggle with her. It had been a delightful way to wake up until she realized there was no way this was going to lead to anything, and it was still dark outside. Half asleep, she'd dressed in jeans, a t-shirt, and sneakers, and threw on one of Ben's old flannel shirts. She wasn't sure it was a good idea to wear jeans in this weather. Ben had reminded her that there were poisonous snakes out here, and the best way she could protect herself was with jeans and closed-in shoes.

When she was following Ben to the combine and walked through the stubble of the stalks where the heads of grain had been removed, she was glad that her legs were covered. The stalks would've scratched her legs, and she didn't even want to think about snake bites.

She even remembered to put on sunscreen before scrunching her hair into a loose bun as Ben was walking out the front door. She didn't even know when he managed to have breakfast. She grabbed a muesli bar on the way out and managed to catch up to him just as he was putting his ute into gear. This harvesting business was serious work. He said something about the slightly cooler weather meant that he could get back to the paddock, and he didn't want to waste any more time.

There had been a slight cooling overnight, and she'd slept like a log. She blushed thinking of the real reason why she'd probably slept well, which had more to do with Ben and the two of them being naked and pleasured than any cool change.

'I'll go around a few times, then you can have a turn." His suggestion broke through her mini daydream.

Blood drained from her face as she computed what he was saying. "You sure?"

"Yeah, it's not that hard."

She didn't believe him. "Maybe go around a dozen

times or so, then I can have a turn." Yesterday she'd been confident about driving the heavy machinery when they'd talked over a BBQ dinner. Now, here, sitting in the cab, the engine roaring with a power she'd never experienced before, she wasn't so sure that this was a good idea.

He laughed and shook his head. "You'll be fine, you've got me as a teacher."

"That's why I'm uncertain."

"Hey, I'll kick you out now, and you can walk back to the farm." His expression was full of amusement.

"I'd like to see you try and kick me out." She found her confidence pushing away the nerves that flooded through her at the mere thought of driving something so big like this combine.

"If only I had the time."

She raised an eyebrow at him in a sort of a mock challenge. "Chicken."

The combine suddenly jerked forward.

Raven let out a short scream, wobbled, arms flying out for something to grab. Her left hand touched the window, and her right wacked Ben on the head.

"Careful."

"Sorry." She managed to regain her balance. It wasn't as if there were anything to hold on to. She narrowed her eyes at Ben. "Was that deliberate?"

"No idea what you're talking about." He looked ahead, then down below, before checking the controls again. Raven was pretty sure he was hiding a grin from her.

"Right, we're good to go. Let's see if we can reap this paddock of wheat today. Hold on."

Raven grabbed hold of Ben, wrapping her arms around his waist, squeezing behind him in the seat, her head on his shoulders.

"Don't hold on to me."

"I really don't know what you expect me to hold on to if it's not you."

He rolled his eyes. "Time to get a little serious."

"Okay." She sat back up, putting her left hand on the glass of the window to steady herself.

"I'll go easy."

"Sure, you will." She didn't think that was in his nature on any level. He was more of a hard-and-fast guy.

Ben eased his foot off the brake, and they jerked forward. Raven nearly slipped off being perched on the arm of the chair.

"Easy, don't bump me. It could end badly."

"Because?"

"See the rotating blades down below? I have to keep an eye on how low it is from the ground, so my hand is on the lever here. You bump me, it could go crashing into the ground. Everything here is expensive, a few extra zeros on the end of it, and I can't afford any breakage."

Raven nodded, pushing her hand into the glass to keep herself from touching Ben. There was no way she wanted to nose dive forward if she bumped him accidentally and whatever it was he'd pointed out to her went into the ground.

It was bumpy driving through the paddock, and she found it hard to keep her balance. "I just need to go up to the crop, then I'll slow down."

"Fine," she muttered, trying to use her leg muscles to stop herself from bouncing into him.

She saw the crop ahead, and as they approached, Ben slowed down. It was easier to find her balance, though she mused how sore her leg muscles were going to be later.

"Better?" he asked.

"Yep." Although now she'd appreciate how comfortable the seating was in her car.

"Just relax, there's nothing to it."

"Sure." She smiled back at Ben. She could tell he was loving having her with him. *Maybe he gets lonely too?* She hadn't thought of that before. How lonely would it be sitting here with no company, even Snipper was back at the house sleeping the day away. Raven might not know exactly the work Ben did on the farm, at least now, but she was becoming more aware of the long hours he was spending alone. Somehow, it eased her feelings of isolation.

Raven leaned back a little to give some of her leg

muscles a rest and engage a different position to stop her from bouncing around. It helped. She couldn't believe how much of a workout she was getting just by trying to sit here and not knock into Ben. Gradually, she found herself settling into the rhythm of the heavy machinery.

Ben kept looking at the controls, lights going on and off, and then looking out the front to give himself a visual. His expression was full of concentration. She wasn't sure how he managed to do this for such long hours during the day for the last few weeks.

Raven looked out through the front window. It was mesmerizing watching the stalks of wheat fold over onto the cutting blades and chopped. It looked effortless. The heads of grain rattled off somewhere else into the machinery, leaving the stalks behind. She understood now why the ends of the stalk were so sharp.

Starting to feel a bit of motion sickness building, she pulled her gaze away, looking out to the horizon. The last thing she wanted to do was to be sick here in the cab and in front of Ben.

The land stretched out in front of her, not entirely flat, but there were some soft, rolling hills, and a scattering of native trees and bushes. The sky was blue and clear of clouds—there wasn't even a wisp of white. The sun shone down, zapping the last bit of green. Her artistic eye saw the different shades of brown that made up the landscape here. She saw the dryness but also the potential, the life in the magpies that flew occasionally in the sky, and in the far distance, she could see some sheep grazing. Paddocks of golden crops immediately surrounded them. There was beauty here, and it felt like she was seeing it for the first time.

Tree lines marked where the dirt roads divided the paddocks and joined the farms. She could just make out wire fences in the distance marking the boundaries between the paddocks.

"Is this all yours?" she asked.

"Not quite, we're a small farm." He pointed to his right. "See the tree line there, that's where our boundary ends."

"The one by the dead-looking old tree?"

"No, the next row of trees, look further up, just below the horizon."

"Oh." She hadn't been looking far enough in the distance. "I see now. So, from there up to the farm is all yours?"

"And my sister's. We share the farm together."

"And your mom." She added, trying not to remember how they were caught by her yesterday.

"That's right. I'll buy my sister out in good time if I can afford it."

Raven's head spun a little. This way of life was so different from what she was used to. She'd never owned her own place, not even a small unit. Here, Ben's family owned acres of land. But then to have to buy his sister out, that would be such a financial burden. There was no inheritance coming to her from her parents. They owned their house, but that was it. It wasn't likely to be something she inherited as she figured they would downsize in the future into an apartment and spend the remaining money traveling around the world.

No wonder there were times he'd looked a little stressed, she thought. Plus, this time of year with the Christmas celebrations must be hard since his father passed a year ago.

"It's just the way it goes," he added. He glanced back at her. "Are you going along all right?"

Raven nodded. She wasn't about to tell him that she was feeling a bit nauseous for sitting in this confined space along with the movement, or that her mind was overwhelmed with processing how life was as a farmer.

Could I adjust? She hated how the questions came to mind, pushing the uncertainty to the surface for consideration.

Ben steered the harvester around to the left, keeping the combine full of the crop so as not to miss any and marking the completion of one round of the paddock. Raven slipped a bit on the arm of the chair but managed not to hit Ben.

The paddock was a huge rectangular shape, and

they were now going along the longer length. She couldn't believe how long it took to do one round. They were, after all, going very slowly, so she felt every bump they drove over. Bouncing around with the movement was surprisingly tiring. At least Ben had a somewhat comfortable chair with suspension.

"What about you have a go?"

"What? Now?" She looked at him, wide-eyed. "You'd really trust me to drive this combine, which is worth... how much money?"

There was no way he could trust her this much.

"Sure. I mean you're not going to try and do any damage, are you?"

"No, of course not."

"Then I'll finish to the end to this section where it's easier to stop, and we can swap positions."

Raven inhaled slowly. This was a huge responsibility. Despite the trepidation of driving something so big and expensive while harvesting the very valuable crop, excitement began to surge through her.

Just wait until I tell my parents this. Raven also figured it would be a good test for her to see if she would be able to adapt to farming life or not. Even though she was pretty sure if there were a long-term future with Ben, it wasn't likely she was going to be on the combine like this. She wanted to try new things, and more importantly, she wanted to understand what it was like for Ben when he was working alone on the farm.

"Ready?"

"Yes." She grinned, now eager to get into the driver's seat.

Ben slowed the machine down so they could swap positions. "Just wait until I stop."

Raven glanced outside. Something along the horizon caught her attention. A knot formed in her belly.

"Is that smoke?" she asked, a chill moving through her body.

"Probably just dust from someone driving too fast along the road."

Raven squinted her eyes. "But it's not on a tree line."

Ben looked up. "Fuck."

He automatically slowed down. "That's old Brumbies' place, I think, but hard to tell from here."

Ben took out his cell. "Jason, there's smoke from Brumbies. Yeah, yeah, I can help with the CFS unit. I'm in the paddock now, the one out to the side of the house. Yeah, that one. I've got the ute with me. Sure, I'll meet you there."

Raven had so many questions to ask, but she kept quiet. Ben was cool and calm, but she could tell he was worried. Lines creased his forehead as he turned the harvester out of the crop, then pushing it to full speed.

"I'll park the harvester by the ute, and I'll have to drive it down to the fire. It's got the water unit on the back, which I'll need until the bigger CFS units arrive." Ben had explained to her at the start of the harvest that the water unit he'd put on the back of the ute was important in case there was a fire.

"Will you be all right to walk back to the house?" asked Ben.

"I can come with you? I can help?"

"No, you're not trained."

She bit back the words 'and you are.' "I can help you."

"You can by going back to the house and staying safe. Fires are unpredictable around here, and there's so much dry material to catch alight. I'm part of the country fire station, CFS, and Jason and the other boys will need my help. With any luck, the fire will be out quickly."

Ben stopped the harvester by the truck and ute. He turned to her, his eyes full of worry. He put his hand on her arm. "You know the way back to the farm?"

Raven nodded her head. "Yes."

He stood up and opened the door for her to get out. Raven paused, not wanting to leave him or to walk back to the farm by herself. This was an emergency. Ben was stepping up, and she would too.

CHAPTER 7

"There's a fire," Raven yelled as she rushed into the farmhouse, the screen door slammed behind her.

"Over at Brumbies." She puffed hard. It had taken her a good twenty minutes to run back to the farm. She'd kept to the road, scared of stepping on a snake or getting lost if she had taken a shortcut through the paddocks.

She hurried into the kitchen, which was always the first place to look for Janette.

"I know."

Raven stopped short in the doorway, bent over a little, hands on her knees as she tried to catch her breath. "Oh."

Janette stood by the kitchen table, arm wrapped around a big bowl, stirring a mixture with a wooden spoon. She wore a summer dress—plain light blue, short sleeves, and A-line skirt that went below her knees—covered with a blue apron, dusted with flour, her gray hair tied back in a long plait that went down her back with wisps of hair coming out. Her expression was cold, her jaw set as she concentrated on whatever she was mixing.

"It's over at Brumbies," continued Janette. She set the bowl on the table, changed her grip, then poured the mixture into a rectangular baking tin.

"Should we go there? Ben might need help?" Raven went over to the fridge and got out the container of cold water. She poured herself a glass and drank almost half, which helped to cool her down.

"They know what they're doing. It's best if we stay out of it," said Janette, her tone matter-of-fact.

"There's nothing we can do, then?" Raven didn't believe it. "There must be some way we can help.

Janette looked up at her. For the first time, Raven saw the worry that Janette was hiding. "Bake. Those fighting the fire will need food."

Raven rolled her lips, holding back the words that she couldn't bake. There were bigger worries playing in her mind. She returned the container of water to the fridge.

"Will they be fighting the fire for long?" asked Raven. Not sure if she wanted to know the answer.

"I hope not." Janette opened the oven door and slid

in the baking tin. A burst of heat entered the room, adding to the heat.

"Ben thought maybe it would be under control quickly." Raven wondered if that was perhaps more wishful thinking on his behalf. "Maybe that means a few hours?"

Janette shook her head. "Who knows." She took a labored breath, one heavy with anxiety.

"I'm sure it will." Raven felt a tightness in her belly. "We don't have to get them food just yet. Let's wait a little while for more news."

"I just have a bad feeling about this." Janette's voice sounded distant.

"I'm sure it will be fine." Raven tried to think of a distraction, despite feeling lost at what to do.

I have to help. I want to help, she corrected herself.

Janette's expression was one of burden.

Raven had an idea. "How about I help you cook. You know I'm really not much of a baker, and I reckon it would be a good idea for me to learn."

Janette looked at her, surprised. "You were going to cook dinner tomorrow. Should I be worried to have agreed to that?"

Raven smiled, glad her comment was proving to be the distraction she'd hoped it would be. "Course not, as long as you're happy not to have dessert on a Sunday night."

"That would be breaking a very long tradition, and we can't have that."

Raven saw the worry ease a little on Janette's face. "What do you suggest I cook then?"

"Hmmm, let's try an apple crumble. There are a few apples in the fridge I need to use."

"Yum, let's get started."

***

"Do you think they'll be home soon?" Raven looked at the clock on the wall for the hundredth time. It was two in the afternoon. The apples were stewed and now cooling, and the crumble made ready to go on top. It had been a lot easier than Raven thought, and she had to admit that Janette was a patient teacher.

Janette shrugged her shoulders. "I have a bad feeling."

"I'll go look outside." Raven got up from peeling the potatoes for the shepherd's pie they were now making for tomorrow night's meal. A much better option than the curries she'd contemplated making.

"It won't help," said Janette.

"I know, but I feel so helpless."

The kitchen was hot with the oven on for so long. Raven had dragged an extra floor-standing fan from the lounge into the room to try and help at least keep the air flowing. She reminded herself that those fighting the fire would be hotter than she was right now.

Cooking was providing a good distraction, but the worry was always there every time she saw Janette's facial expression. At this rate, they were going to have the meals cooked and ready for Christmas.

"Get some fresh air, then."

Raven stepped outside. Straightaway, she could smell the smoke. A haunting foreboding shivered through her. She walked out from the shade of the veranda, and the heat felt like it was physically pressing down on her. The wind whipped up around her as if playing with the dust. It was an awful day and a bad day for fires. That's what Janette had said. It hadn't started like this, and she'd never noticed how quickly the weather could turn. It never really mattered to her when living in the city. There were the sounds of the emergency services, but that was as far as her concern went. Here, she didn't know old Brumbie, but Janette and Ben did, and if his place were on fire, they were worried.

She scanned the horizon. To her left was a sinister billowing cloud of smoke, smearing across the sky. It felt close. Too close. Janette had assured her that there were miles between here and Brumbie's place, and the wind was coming from the north, blowing the fire away from them. The smell of life burning in the air and seeing the clouds of smoke haunting the sky, she felt the fire was too close for comfort.

She sighed, knowing that coming out hadn't helped, and Janette had been right. Looking out to the horizon in the direction of the fire had only stirred her anxiety, giving it more fuel. She longed to call Ben on his cell and make sure that he was all right. But, of course, Raven didn't. He needed to concentrate, and she didn't want to distract him. His life could well depend on it.

It was even too early for the eggs to be collected and hay given to the alpacas. With nothing else to do, she went back inside. Rex scampered inside between her legs.

"Damn cat," called Janette from the kitchen.

"I'll get him out," said Raven.

"No, don't worry, he can have some time inside. If we need to evacuate, at least we'll know where he is."

"Evacuate?" Her mouth dried. Would they really have to?

"I'm sure it won't come to that." Janette took a deep breath. "Cup of tea?"

"Please." Raven sat down at the table, playing with her cell, wishing she could call Ben to be sure he was okay.

"Don't worry, bad news travels fast," said Janette as she set a cup of tea in front of Raven.

"Is it always like this?" Raven's mind whirled through a sea of emotions flooding through her.

"Like what?"

"Waiting like this."

"You're always waiting on the ones you love when you're a farmer's wife."

Raven nodded. It was what she was beginning to think would happen.

No wonder she cooks a lot.

There wasn't much else to do. The internet wasn't working well, but that was good because she could see herself constantly looking for updates about the fire to see if anything had gone wrong.

Raven shook her head. She was starting to feel sick having to wait like this. Was this her future waiting at this kitchen table for Ben?

Can I do this?

* * *

RAVEN LAY AWAKE IN BED. Moonlight filtered in the room through the small window to the left, helping her to see a little. She looked up at the ceiling making out the movement of the fan going around. It moved the warm air making the heat tolerable. She kicked at the cotton sheet covering her, pushing it down in a tangled mess to the end of the bed. She wore a singlet and panties, and for the first time was beginning to wish there was an air conditioner to turn on.

She flung a hand out to her right and was about to say sorry when she remembered Ben wasn't back yet. He was still out fighting the fire. Or as Janette hoped was the case, he might simply be staying out watching the area in case it flared up again.

Raven tilted her head back to look at the bedside clock. It was past midnight. She moved her arm back and forth, wishing that Ben was there. Out of habit, she picked up her phone lying near her. There was still no message or call from him. How she wished there was. Just a quick text to say he was all right. Even if he were fighting a fire, surely, he would have time to do that?

She rolled over, settling in the middle of the bed. When he came home, she wanted him to wake her.

Raven had reluctantly gone to bed. Janette left a plate of food in the fridge for Ben with a note on the table. Raven had stayed up a little longer, but she couldn't stand watching any more of the late-night television or even another DVD. She didn't want to sleep either. The waiting for more news was silently eating away at her.

Her mind swung between thoughts of hoping Ben was okay and wondering if she could tolerate this waiting and the loneliness of living on a farm. The heat lulled her into a restless sleep.

A slight movement of the bed woke her.

"Just me," whispered Ben.

Ben wrapped his body against her. He smelled of smoke mixed with fresh soap, and his hair was a little damp.

"I missed you." Raven turned to look at him. He kissed her. It was smoky, it was salty, and it reassured her that everything was well.

"I'm fine."

Raven sensed the exhaustion in his voice. "The fire is out?"

"Yeah, just a few people staying there watching in case it flares up again."

"Your mom mentioned something about that." She nestled into him, enjoying his body wrapped around hers. "Much damage?"

"Brumbie lost his house and two of his sheds. One was left standing. Some of his sheep, too."

"Fuck, that bad?"

"Yeah."

"What started it?"

"He took an old Massy Ferguson tractor out in the paddock, must've sparked or something, and it took off. At least that's what it looks like. His neighbor on the other side of him lost a paddock of wheat to the fire, too."

"That's terrible."

"I'm glad you and Mom are fine here. We were lucky." He squeezed her tightly.

"What will he do?"

"He's old stock. He'll be fine. We'll all look out for him." His words slurred as Ben started to fall asleep.

Raven kept quiet, letting him get the rest he needed. She felt herself relax. He was all right, and he was finally in bed with her. The waiting was finally over.

CHAPTER 8

Sunday, December 22nd

Raven dreamed there was an annoying fly trapped in the room with her. No matter how much she looked, she couldn't find it.

"Okay, I'll get down there now."

Ben's voice broke the dream, and her eyes fluttered open. He was talking on his cell. She smiled, grateful he was with her. She reached out and ran her hand down his back as he sat up in bed.

"I'll be there in five minutes."

Raven felt a tightness in her chest. His tone was serious. Something was wrong. A selfish side of her wanted to grab him and not let him go. She didn't want him to leave her. It would be nice to have a long sleep-in for a change.

If only that were possible. Another sacrifice for living on a farm.

Ben ended the call, turned, and took her hand in his. "The fire's flared up."

"What?"

"It can happen." His forehead was a wrinkled mess with worry.

She moved to hug him, sitting on her knees. "This isn't good."

"No." He broke the embrace. "I have to get moving. There's no time to waste."

"Can I help?" She watched him get dressed in his usual attire on the farm—jeans and a shirt. His eyes were bloodshot, she assumed from the smoke.

"By staying here."

"I hate waiting."

"There will be more for you to do today. Just stay with Mom. If you have to, I want you two to go into Keith."

"You mean evacuate?"

"If it comes to that."

His serious expression made her skin prickle. She rubbed her arms as if she were cold.

"I mean it, Raven, I want you two to be safe. The farm, the house, those things can all be replaced. You can't be."

Tears welled in her eyes. *This can't be happening.*

"Raven," he said her name softly, stepped back to

the bed toward her. He embraced her, and she held on to him tightly. "I'm sure it won't come to that, but I just want you to be prepared."

She didn't want to think of having to leave because of a fire. That would ruin him and the farm, and she didn't think it would be easy to rebuild from that.

Raven felt his strength boosting her confidence. She had to be strong—by doing so it would help Ben. The last thing she wanted was for him to be worrying about her when he was in a dangerous situation.

"I will, but only if it comes to that." She couldn't believe she managed to speak the words confidently. A shocking realization sent a shiver down her spine.

"Thank you." He kissed her, squeezing her shoulders. His lips were warm on hers and sent a delightful burst of pleasure through her. He broke the kiss slowly.

"I've got to go."

"I'll see you later. You keep yourself safe."

"I will, just for you." He grinned, but his eyes didn't light up with cheekiness.

Raven watched him walk from the room. While the last few days her thoughts were full of doubt about whether she could cope with life on the farm, she just had a small revelation—she didn't think she would be able to walk away from the farm not knowing if she would be able to return.

.   .   .

***

RAVEN WALKED DOWN to the kitchen in search of a strong cup of coffee. She suppressed a yawn as she walked in and rubbed the remaining sleep from her eyes. Surprised Janette wasn't there, she picked up the kettle and took it to the sink. Looking out the window to the backyard as the kettle filled with rainwater, she spied Janette hanging up Ben's work clothes on the clothesline.

That's odd.

She didn't think that it would be a good idea to hang out clothes when there was a fire nearby.

Surely, they'd end up smelling of smoke and would have to be rewashed?

Raven set the kettle to boil, then realized that Janette might not be aware of the fire flaring up. She went outside.

"Morning," called Janette from behind Ben's jeans as she pegged them to the line.

"Morning." Raven paused, sure from the happy tone from Janette that she indeed didn't know.

"Thought you two might enjoy a little sleep-in."

Raven's cheeks brightened with heat. She was still mortified she'd been caught with Ben. Besides, it was only just after seven in the morning, and Raven didn't consider this anything close to a sleep-in by her city standards.

"Where's Ben, anyway?" Janette turned and picked up a red checkered shirt and gave it a sharp flick before pegging it to dry.

"Out fighting the fire."

Janette's face whitened. "But I thought it was out."

Raven shook her head. "He got an early call this morning."

Janette sighed heavily. "This isn't good."

"No."

"Better take these clothes inside then, and here I was thinking I was getting ahead. I'll need to start prepping for Christmas today."

"Let me help." Raven took down Ben's damp jeans and slung them in the laundry basket.

"Thanks." Janette looked stoic as she picked up the basket.

"Here, let me," offered Raven. She was beginning to feel helpless again.

"I've got it. Come on inside. Best start the day with a cup of tea." She put on a brave smile. "Perhaps a coffee for you, though."

Raven tried to smile back, but she was too worried about the fire. Finally, Janette seemed to be getting the hang of her tastes in hot drinks. A small step, but to Raven, it felt significant.

A gush of wind whipped around her, its breath

warm for the morning, yet a chill went through Raven. "Did you feel that?"

"Wind's changed direction."

Raven couldn't shake off that was a bad omen as they returned inside. She went to finish making herself a coffee and got a pot of tea brewing for Janette while she hung the clothes on an airing rack inside. She didn't think she could stomach breakfast this morning as her stomach was a roiling mess of fear and worry. Of the fire. For Ben. Even for Janette. And of course, the farm and the animals.

"I have a tea ready for you," said Raven as Janette came into the kitchen. "Take a seat and rest your legs."

"Thanks, it's going to be another big day of cooking."

Raven nodded her head as she sat down on the kitchen chair opposite Janette. Silence settled between them as they were both lost in their own thoughts and concerns.

The phone rang.

The sound broke through her thoughts causing Raven to jump. Tea sloshed over the edge of her cup. "Dammit."

"I'll get it." Janette got up from sitting at the table with a groan and went to answer the phone set on a small table in the hallway.

Raven reached over for a tea towel and wiped the spilled tea. Her head pounded, and she rubbed her temples trying to get her thoughts to settle. *Was this what her future would be like on the farm?* The loneliness returned with a force, and she struggled to ignore it.

"That was Anne. The fire is a bit of a beast, and the women from the CWA are getting some food together for those fighting the fire." Her voice was thick with worry as she came back into the kitchen.

"CWA?"

"Country Women's Association." Janette opened the fridge door and began taking out food—cold cuts of meat, lettuce, and tomato.

Raven wondered if Janette was sugar-coating things for her. "That sounds bad."

"I'm sure they will get it under control before dark. What we need to do is to make some sandwiches, but I'm out of bread."

"I'll go into town. Tell me what you need me to get," Raven said. At least the trip into Keith would help her feel like she was actually doing something to help.

"I'll write out a list for you."

CHAPTER 9

ist in hand, Raven drove carefully into Keith. Every time she glanced in the rearview mirror, she could see a glimpse of the smoke from the fire. It was weird carrying on like this, knowing that at least Brumbie had lost his home and some of his stock, and now with the flare-up, there could be more loss.

Raven focused on driving as she turned down the main street of Keith. It was early, eight o'clock, but the supermarket was open. She went straight there and worked systematically through the list Janette had written for her. It felt like she was buying enough food to feed an army.

Loading the car with the bags of food, she looked up the street. She still hadn't gotten Ben a gift. Now wasn't really the time, but since the shops were opening and Janette told her to be back by ten, she thought a little retail distraction might help get her mind off of how Ben was doing.

I'll hurry. Considering she had no idea what to get him, she wasn't sure this quick shop would result in a gift. If she didn't look now, she wasn't sure she'd get a gift for him before Christmas. Since this was their first Christmas together, she wanted to have something meaningful to give him.

Better I get this gift now.

Raven started walking along the main street, trying to decide which store might yield the perfect Christmas gift for Ben. Not only didn't she have a lot of time to indulge in gift shopping, there wasn't much choice here in Keith in terms of shops.

There was a Mitre Ten hardware store behind her, but she had no idea what tools he might need on the farm.

The JK Jewelers' store sign ahead caught her attention. He wasn't the sort of man who wore jewelry. She'd even noticed that the men didn't wear their wedding rings, and when she asked, she was told it was for safety. There were a few stories of men getting the rings caught in machinery and losing a finger at best or part of their arm at worst.

Her heart squeezed a little with disappointment. She'd always imagined her man would wear their wedding ring. But then again, things were different and hadn't gone to plan by falling in love with a farmer. She'd rather he was alive than risk his life wearing a wedding ring. She surprised herself with such thoughts. With all the doubt whirling in her mind, here she was thinking that they were going to get married. She wished it would put away the feeling of loneliness from living on the farm, but it didn't.

Raven walked past the bank. Ben had told her they were lucky to have one in town since many of the big banks were pulling out of the smaller towns. Though Keith was considered one of the bigger country townships around here, which meant they had a bank, a school, and even a library. But no hospital.

There was the local pharmacy, which also had a section for gifts. Raven kept walking, thinking that there had to be a better option.

"How are you, Raven? That's not good about that fire," said Mrs. Peterson as she approached her. She pushed a walker. She used to be Ben's primary school teacher, and one person she'd met a few times when in town with Ben. She liked that she tried not to remember just her but also speak with her.

"No, I hope they get it out soon." Ben had told her how she was one of the few teachers who had stayed in the area when they came here to teach, only because she'd married a local farmer.

"I'm sure they will. I need to get up to the CWA. We're making some sandwiches for those at the fire."

Mrs. Peterson continued on, pushing her walker to keep her steady on her feet.

"I'm helping Janette get some ready, too."

Mrs. Peterson nodded. "That sounds like Janette. I'll see you later."

"Bye." The reminder of the fire twisted at her stomach. *I should go home now.*

But for some reason, she stayed and looked down the street at the line of shops. There weren't a lot of options, and she didn't want to make do for Ben's present. Besides, since there weren't so many shops, it wouldn't take long to have a look at what she might be able to get him.

If only I had time to go to Adelaide. She would've perhaps bought something online if she knew it would arrive on time. It was too close to Christmas now, and since she lived away from a major city, it was likely to arrive too late.

A reflection on a sign caught her attention—Heart and Soul Gifts. The gift shop was new to the area, and one that Raven wasn't familiar with. She pushed on the front door and walked in, deciding it was as good a place as any.

Incense wafted to her as she walked inside, the smell evoking a sense of peace for her. The place was organized and neat. There were small round tables with long white cloths over them scattered around the shop. Some had candles, some fancy glass, and others had little statues of unicorns, which she really didn't think were at all suitable as a gift for Ben.

She picked up a coconut and lime scented candle and smelled it. This could be all right for Anne. She kept it in her hand as she wandered around the shop, looking.

Raven spied some wooden, handmade items on a lower shelf along the wall. They were made from jarrah wood. There was a bowl, which she thought would be suitable for Janette. A tube which was labeled 'pencil case,' which she thought was a cool idea but, of course, not a suitable present for Ben.

For some reason, she kept looking through the carved objects. One, in particular, caught her attention.

Just what I was looking for.

She picked it up and turned it over in her hand. She wanted the gift to be special, to have meaning that was between her and Ben.

Her heartbeat skipped. *But would he like it?*

"Can I help you?" the young female shop assistant came up to Her. "I'm Nat."

"Do you do gift wrapping?" she asked, knowing that there was no way she'd manage to find the time to wrap this gift, not with the fire. She realized they hadn't even put up the Christmas tree yet. The fire was putting everything out of alignment.

Unsure if Ben would appreciate, let alone like this gift, she handed it to Nat. Most guys were used to getting jocks and socks, and she wondered if while predictable, if that's what she should do. At least it would cause him to have a laugh. She looked at the carving in her hand. For whatever reason, this felt right. This had a special meaning that she couldn't get past.

"Can you please wrap it for me?"

"Of course, Christmas paper?"

"Yes, and can you wrap the candle and bowl as well?"

"Sure thing."

"Thanks." Raven remembered she needed Christmas cards. She made her way over to the rack of cards. They were stock standard cards, and what she wanted was unique cards to make this Christmas together with his family special.

I could design my own, and the thought amused her. If there weren't the fire and more time before Christmas, making her own cards could be easy. But this thought came from somewhere deeper. It wasn't a fleeting idea, but something she could do alongside her online business, and with any luck, it might well take off.

Something to consider later. Raven went to the counter to pay and collect the wrapped gifts. If anything, thinking about making her cards might just help her stop worrying about Ben.

· · ·

* * *

JANETTE AND RAVEN set up a production line of sandwich-making in the kitchen. Raven couldn't believe she was helping to make five dozen sandwiches. It wasn't even midday yet.

The kitchen table had the bread lined up in neat columns, two slices of bread next to each other for the sandwich. The bread covered most of the space. She was going through smearing butter on them. Janette then followed with a slice of cold meat, corn beef or ham or chicken, followed with a piece of lettuce, and then a piece of tomato. Raven finished by smearing tomato chutney on one side of the sandwich and closed them up. Janette finally cut them diagonally making two large triangles.

"What do I package them into?"

"On the top shelf of the cupboard there are some big plastic containers," said Janette, not even looking up from cutting the sandwich.

Raven opened the large kitchen cupboard and went up on her tiptoes. She could just reach the containers. Carefully, she pulled them down. They were huge. It wasn't something she'd ever thought to have in her kitchen. It appeared that when things were done out here, they were done on a much bigger scale.

Raven wiped out the containers, then set them on a

chair and started stacking the sandwiches inside them. They fit perfectly. She knew that Janette had put thought into what containers she was buying and the size. She wouldn't have. She was impressed.

She placed the lid on the container, set it over by the counter space near the kettle, and began filling another.

"I think we should take them to the fire front," said Janette.

"You think? Didn't you say that they were setting up a place for volunteers to rest in Keith?" As much as Raven wanted to see Ben, she also remembered how firm he was that she stayed here.

"I did," Janette replied firmly. "I'll fill up some bottles of water to take as well, and that should tie them over for a bit."

Raven saw the stern look on Janette's face and didn't dare argue with her. "I'll drive, you tell me where to go."

"Okay, let's get going, then."

It took two trips each to get the containers of sandwiches and bottles of water in the back of Raven's car.

Her knuckles whitened from the tight grip she had on the steering wheel as she drove along the driveway to the public road.

"Turn right here," instructed Janette. "It's not hard to get to Brumbies."

"Is that where they'll be?"

"I'm not sure, but we'll soon find out."

"Should you ring Ben first and see exactly where they are?"

"No."

Raven couldn't help thinking that there was something else going on here for Janette. Maybe she wanted to make sure Ben was safe and sound too. She kept driving, slowly along the dirt road, her belly fluttering with nerves knowing she was driving toward the fire.

They sat in silence. The smoke billowing into the sky gradually came closer. Raven felt herself holding her breath, and she had to force herself to exhale, then inhale. She crouched forward over the steering wheel.

"Are those flames up ahead?" She squinted, trying to work out if she were now seeing the fire or not. Despite the heat, her skin prickled. She wanted to see Ben, make sure he was fine, but at the same time, the urge to turn around to flee was increasing.

"Oh my," gasped Janette.

The land flattened out, giving them both a full view of the fire and the damage it had done. Flames flickered in the distance, but for Raven, it felt way too close.

"You sure I should keep going?"

Janette didn't answer. She sat, hand on her mouth, eyes wide, staring out at the scene in front of them. Tears fell down her cheeks. Flames licked their way up the trunks of the trees either side of the road, the crop that had proudly been standing in its golden glory was now burned to nothing, ash heavy on the ground.

To her right, Raven saw a CFS unit, hoses pulled from the back of the truck, men and women holding them and putting out spot fires, trying to stop it from spreading.

Then she saw Ben.

She stopped the car.

Ben was covered in black soot. Even though he was over a hundred feet away, she could see the worried look on his face. He held the hose tightly, water spurting out, barely smothering the flames.

Raven turned her gaze to where he was facing. Right then, the wind whipped around them shaking the car.

"Fuck."

The strength of the wind created a fire twister. Flames snaked up in a rope-like fashion from the ground up into the sky. Its tip danced on the ground for seconds, moving along to the right, it's beauty and terrifying nature captivating Raven. It sparked something inside of her. Seeing the fire twister in all its distressing flames, burned through her doubt. All the thoughts that had been tumbling around in her head wanting answers collided, and she finally knew.

There were two directions she could take—go back to city life or stay. But there was only *one* answer.

Fear swept through her seeing the monstrous fire

out of control. The answer still remained clear. Here, seeing the snake of fire rising from the ground, she knew the answer in her bones. She was staying. Life out here in the country wasn't what she was used to, but she knew she could adjust. To live here and be happy as long as Ben was with her. Right now, she was choosing farm life, and one way or another, she would deal with the loneliness because her home was here now. She felt her roots go down. She was not just with Ben, they would be together with their own family in the future. And that's what she wanted.

Raven's realization didn't stop there. Her stomach fluttered with excitement. Realization flooded through her. She would give the club idea a go. Hell, she might even cook a cake in Janette's kitchen by herself to sell on a fundraising table. It wasn't so much she had to, but she wanted to. Because of Ben. It wasn't as if she were changing for him, only adapting. One thing was becoming clear for her, and that was she owed it to him, to herself, for them both, and for the sake of the future children they would have.

With the decision of how she wanted her future with Ben, here in the country, her mind snapped back to reality.

"Shit, we need to get out of here." She put the car in reverse. Looked back at Ben as he turned to face them. His face was a mix of surprise and then anger. He mouthed 'go.'

Raven didn't need him to repeat it. She should've argued with Janette, stood up to her, but things had been going so well between them, they were bonding, getting to know each other, that she hadn't wanted to do anything that might upset that delicate balance.

Quickly, she reversed her car, turned around, and high-tailed it back to the farm. The further they got away from the fire, the easier it was to breathe, but the tension remained with her.

The fire was too close to the farm for her liking.

***

THE PHONE RANG AS SOON as Janette and Raven walked into the farmhouse. Janette sprung to life and rushed to get it.

"Anne, yes, I'll come in with the sandwiches."

Raven knew damn well that's where they should've gone in the first place. She knew now. She hoped Ben wasn't going to be too upset with her. Worry kept her stomach in knots.

"No, we'll stay here." Janette abruptly hung up the phone and stomped back down to the kitchen.

"I'm putting the kettle on."

It was Janette's solution to everything. Raven wanted to know what made her so upset when she felt the buzz of her cell. She took it out of her pocket. There was a message from Ben, her heart quickened, thumping hard in her chest as she read the message. Her hands shook.

This can't be happening.

Raven read the message again.

> Fires out of control, it's coming your way. Get Mom and go into town. NOW.

"WE'RE GOING INTO TOWN." Raven looked at Janette.

"No, I'm staying here. I'm going to fight. I'm not going to let a bloody fire destroy all the hard work my husband did before he died..." Her words choked in tears.

"Leaving won't destroy that. Your life is more important." Raven suspected that might've been what the call was about. They were told to leave. She took a deep breath, trying to find the words quickly to motivate her to get in the car. She'd seen the flames and knew that there was no way she had the means to fight back.

"This is what Ben wants, and you know he's fine. Don't make him worry." She typed back a message to Ben.

.   .   .

Leaving now.

Janette took a deep breath.

Raven cut her off. "You saw how bad it was out there just now. We have a car full of food, and I can only guess that there are people who'll need your help in town. Get in the car now." Raven put her hands on her hips.

Janette paused, closing her eyes as she took a deep breath.

Raven's mind raced and wondered how things would go if she went up to Jeanette and grabbed her arm and tried to drag her back to the car. She was beginning to get worried, Janette was going to be bloody stubborn.

"I'll grab Rex."

Raven breathed, her pulse racing. "Hurry."

She stepped outside, fighting the urge to go back inside to grab her things. What was going to happen to the alpacas? And Evie? Her own eyes began to water with emotion.

She coughed from the smoke in the air as she rushed with Janette to the car. She held on to Rex, who by some miracle was calm.

Snipper ran up to them, and Raven opened the back seat for him to jump in. She'd put all the alpacas in there too if they would fit, and if they had time. It felt like they had no time. She glanced up the road where they had driven before. Not only could she see the smoke but also the flames. There was only one way out of the farm in her city car.

"Quickly." She opened the door, glad that Janette could get in on her own even though she was holding the cat. She figured things might go south with the cat and the dog in the car, but there was an eerie silence inside as she slammed her door.

Usually, she would drive carefully along the unsealed driveway. For the first time, she put her foot down on the accelerator, ignoring the bumps, and drove as fast as she dared. Her heart was squeezing, hoping against the odds there would be a home and alpacas for her to return to.

CHAPTER 10

Monday, December 23rd

Raven barely had any sleep. She and Janette had gone into Keith, where fortunately Anne had met them, and helped to calm Janette, reassuring her that they had to leave the farm. They had spent the rest of the day helping prepare food for the people fighting the fire. All the time Raven had thought about whether or not the place she was beginning to call home had burned down or not.

At dusk, Anne said that they would come back to her place. Raven didn't mind the option of sleeping on the couch. Life was much better than material possessions. She just hoped that the alpacas were safe and sound. Rex was making himself at home at Anne's, and Snipper was his usual happy self, claiming the backyard as his own.

Raven texted Ben to say where they were and that they were safe. He snuck into Anne's place in the early hours of the morning exhausted, smelling of smoke and covered in ash. He could barely string a sentence together, so Raven had let him fall asleep in a pile of blankets on the floor next to the couch that was her bed for the night. She didn't know if the farm were safe or not, or if Evie was alive, and it made it harder to sleep, along with the incredibly uncomfortable couch. Despite all of that, she must've managed to fall asleep, at least for a little while.

The sound of someone in the kitchen, the kettle boiling, and the clinking of plates on the table caused Raven to wake. Enough light filtered out from the kitchen allowing her to see a little, even though the light coming in between the cracks at the edge of the blind suggested that the sun had definitely risen for the day. She looked over to see Ben sound asleep.

He stirred, eyes fluttering as if they were deciding whether or not to face the day.

"Hey," said Raven when he turned his head and looked at her. He groaned as if hungover. His eyes were bloodshot, and soot was smeared on his face.

"I better get back out there." He groaned again as he sat up.

"I think you need more rest." She sat up on the edge of the couch, her bare feet touching the carpeted floor.

"Not until the fire is out."

"But..."

He put up his hand to stop her, shook his head, then got up from where he'd been sleeping on the floor.

"You worried me by coming to the fire yesterday."

"I'm sorry. Your mom wanted to drop off some food. I couldn't stop her... I wanted to see you."

He took a long, deep breath as if trying to clear his lungs.

There was a burning question she had to ask. "Are the alpacas... is Evie..."

"They're fine."

She breathed out heavily. "Thank God."

"The fire came close, though."

"How close?" She swallowed hard and braced herself for whatever Ben was going to tell her.

"You'll understand when you see the place."

"Can I go there today?"

"I don't think so. There were people stationed around there during the night to keep a watch if there were any flare-ups. It would be safer if you stayed in Keith, at least until you hear otherwise."

It would be safer if you didn't go and fight the fire, but she didn't say those words. Of course, he had to go. She couldn't believe how people were coming together and helping out.

Raven stood up and wrapped her arms around his

waist. He smelled of smoke and sweat, and she didn't care. She was glad to be able to put her arms around him and to hold him. He squeezed her tightly, and she rested her head on his chest. She didn't want to let him go. It would mean he would be going back to the fire and put his life in danger again.

"It scared the hell out of me seeing you there, so close to the fire," his voice soft in her ear. She tightened her grip around his waist, pulling him as close as possible to her.

"I don't know what I'd do if anything happened to you," he added. His words caused her eyes to fill with tears and were heartening to hear—a reassurance especially after she had made up her mind for once and all that she was going to be a farm girl and no longer a city girl.

Raven blinked quickly, just stopping the tears from falling. She looked up at him. As much as she hated to have to let him go, she knew she had to.

"Stay safe. I have your Christmas gift, and I want to be able to give it to you," said Raven.

He smiled at her. His eyes were tired, worried, looked directly into hers. "I look forward to opening it on Christmas Day." He kissed her, a brief, smoky touch on her lips, and then he left.

* * *

. . .

RAVEN'S HEART squeezed painfully knowing that he'd gone back to the fire. She sat at the kitchen table, instant coffee in front of her, along with Janette and Anne.

Ben's absence was noticeable and a sign that the fire was still burning.

"Ready to make some more sandwiches?" asked Janette.

"Absolutely." Raven took a sip of her coffee. "Though I must admit that I don't think I'll be able to make another sandwich, let alone even eat one after this."

"I know what you mean," said Janette. She tried to smile. "I'm sorry I should've known better than to get you to drive to the fire and refuse to leave."

"We got through it," said Raven, smiling at Janette. "And we better get on with these sandwiches."

"I'll get the bread lined up," offered Anne.

"Do we have enough bread?" asked Raven.

"I've already been to the supermarket," said Anne.

Raven felt a little bad that she'd been left sleeping. "You should've woken me."

"It didn't take long. Come on, we should get these sandwiches made and over to the town hall."

With the three of them pitching in to help, it didn't take long for the sandwiches to be made and packed.

Raven drove them to the town hall. For the second day, she set about helping to make sure there was food to be eaten, and the urn boiled so people could make a hot drink.

At least the weather today was a bit cooler.

Raven saw an older man sitting by himself, looking sad.

"Want me to get you a cup of tea?" asked Raven.

He shook his head.

"I'm Raven." She sat down next to him.

"Brumbie."

"Oh, I'm so sorry." She remembered Ben saying that he'd lost his home in the fire. It was just him on the farm, his son deciding not to stay and lived overseas in London working in some high-powered job.

"You and me both," he mumbled.

"Will you rebuild?"

"I'm too old for that. Only one shed survived the fire, and all that's in there is a rusty old printer and some old farm equipment that's worth nothing."

"A printer?" Raven remembered the odd idea of making her own cards yesterday.

"It's not good, run by hand, rusted to buggery, made in 1903."

"Why did you have it?"

"Bought it in an auction about thirty years ago. My boy was interested in printing, or so I thought. I had hoped we could restore it together, but he had the city lights in his eyes and left as soon as he could."

A crazy idea formed in her head. This could be a chance for her to help Brumbie and also add another stream to her graphic design business. *Would he be up for the challenge?*

"Could you restore it now?"

"I reckon I could, but there's no point. There's no one to use it."

"I could use it."

She smiled, seeing the surprised look on his face.

"You?"

"I want to print my own cards. Could this printer do the job?"

"Old Marg could do the job, but it will take a bit of work for that to happen."

"Old Marg?"

"That's her name."

Raven liked to see how his face was beginning to come alive. "That's a good name for a printer from the 1900s. I could help you restore it if you like."

Brumbie paused, rubbing his prickly chin from the beard growth. "You know, this could work. I'm going to have to live in town now, and I don't want to. But this, finally getting to bring life back to Old Marg could be a good hobby for me."

"Good."

"You know what? I've got a few other old machines in that bloody shed."

"Now you've got the time, looks like you're going to be very busy."

He smiled at her. "Thank you."

"For what?"

"For the great suggestion to..." He shrugged his shoulders. His eyes went watery. "Just thank you."

"My pleasure, and you know I'm completely serious about using Old Marg and printing cards. I don't know if I'll make any money."

"Money is overrated." He winked at her. "I'll have you helping me. You know, Ben's a very lucky man."

Raven giggled. It felt good not to be so heavy with worry. "I'm pretty lucky to have him, I think."

"Raven," Janette yelled out her name sharply.

Panic rose inside of Raven, and she turned to see Ben's mom hurrying toward her.

"The fire..."

Raven held her breath. *No.*

"It's all fine... they've given us the all-clear to go home."

Home. Raven smiled as a tear slid down her cheek. She could finally go home.

***

·   ·   ·

Ben drove his ute along the driveway, the sight of his home, more comforting than he ever remembered. They had done it. All of them worked hard to keep the flames from destroying his farm and keeping his alpacas safe. But it wasn't without loss. Or damage. The fire had come close to their home, marked by the burned areas, some only a few yards from the house. One of the wheat paddocks was lost in the fire, the valuable grain burned and scattered to ash instead.

He parked the ute and was happy to see that the shed was still standing and hadn't been destroyed. He got out and was given a hero's welcome by Snipper jumping on him, tail wagging over excitedly. He patted him, glad his dog was safe. He just had to see Raven. He reeked of sweat and smoke, but he wanted to take her in his arms and simply hold her.

Ben knew just where to find her.

He strode down to the alpacas. There she was, leaning on the fence, watching them. He smiled to himself. She wore shorts and a shirt, hair blowing in the warm afternoon light breeze. The sight of her in the light of the setting sun was the only comfort he needed.

Raven suddenly turned around. She smiled, her eyes lit up with relief. "Ben."

He rushed toward her, scooped her into his arms, and spun her around.

"It's over?" she asked.

He kissed her hard on the lips, enjoying every bit of finally being about to do so.

Ben nodded, placing her on the ground. They might've lost a crop, and money was going to be super tight for the next year, maybe even two years. He didn't care. All that mattered was that he could hold Raven in his arms.

CHAPTER 11

Tuesday, December 24th

"Will it always be like this?" Raven asked as she began washing the dirty dishes in the sink. She'd been helping Janette prepare the Christmas turkey ready to start cooking in the morning.

"Having this many people over for Christmas?"

Raven wasn't sure how they were going to feed so many people. Anne and her boyfriend were outside setting up tables and chairs which they'd borrowed from the town hall. Brumbie wasn't the only one to lose his house, a young family with two young girls also lost everything. They were all coming here for Christmas Day lunch.

"No, Ben on the harvester when it's Christmas tomorrow."

"Yes, we don't often manage to get the harvest finished before Christmas."

Raven didn't mind. At least there were still paddocks for Ben to reap. They came too close to being burned in the fire.

"I've been thinking," said Janette suddenly.

"About what?"

"I'm moving out."

Raven fumbled with the cup she was washing at the sink, just managing to hold the grip so it didn't break. "What?"

"You heard me. I'm moving out."

"You can't." Raven blurted out the words. This was the last thing she wanted. Now. A few days ago, she would've celebrated. So much had changed so quickly with the fires. Raven had seen what it meant to be part of a community and a family, all sticking together no matter what.

"I can so."

"I don't want you to."

"You two love birds need your space."

Raven hoped she wasn't blushing at those words. "I'm sorry about the other day. It won't happen again."

"But it will."

Fuck it better not, thought Raven.

"This is your home, and you're staying," said Raven.

"But you and Ben, well... you two need privacy."

"We'll just have to go on holidays, then."

"Planning on going on a lot of them, are you?"

Raven quickly turned away to grab the dirty plates so Janette wouldn't see the shock mixed with blushing on her face. Janette had a way of sharpshooting to the point, that was for sure. Raven grinned to herself, realizing she was getting used to it instead of being offended.

"If my graphic designs take off."

"Better hope they take off then, you'll need the money."

"Damn right." Raven smiled as she looked Janette straight in the eye. "So, it's settled then. You're staying and never moving out."

"Let's not say never."

"Why?"

"Makes me think of dying."

"Oh." She let the plate she was washing drop back into the water with a soapy splash and forced Janette into an embrace. "You're much too young to think of that."

Janette scoffed, and Raven squeezed her tighter.

"Besides, I don't want Ben blaming me if you move out."

"He won't. I'll tell him."

Raven sighed, releasing her from the hug. "You're not bloody moving out. There's plenty of room for the three of us here."

"You want me to stay as a third wheel."

Raven looked her in the eyes. "I want you to stay as my mom."

"Oh." Janette's eyes welled with tears. "Oh."

Raven got up and embraced Janette. There was a noise behind her, and she turned to see Ben.

"Mom, are you crying? I was worried the fires might be too much," said Ben.

Janette quickly stepped back and used the edge of her tea towel she was holding to wipe the corners of her eyes. "Raven just made me very happy."

Ben strode over to Raven and hugged her. "She has a way of doing that."

Raven secretly grinned to herself, nestling into Ben. She had finally rendered Janette speechless.

CHAPTER 12

Christmas Day

Wednesday, December 25th

The shared Christmas lunch had been a success. The sun shone hot and high in the cloudless sky, making everyone drowsy from overeating.

Brumbie had given Raven a detailed outline of the timeline he'd already worked out to get Old Marg up and running and back to her former glory. She was glad a simple idea had helped him to connect with life and not despair after losing so much in the fire. Who knew if there would be any money in printing her own cards, but it meant that she was getting to know a local, and the idea was giving him a reason to live. That's all that really mattered to her. Raven felt like she was beginning to be part of this community. The loneliness still lingered, but now it was under the surface, and it didn't haunt her as it had only days ago. She knew it was something she could handle. Now and in the future.

"How do you like your first Christmas on the farm?" asked Ben coming up to her with his gift in hand. She lay on the little section of grass that hadn't been burned by the fire.

"It's perfect." She sat up.

"High standards for next year, then?" he said as he sat next to her. It felt good to have him close to her again and not in danger fighting the fire.

"Yes."

His grin broadened. "You mean you're happy to be here for another year?"

"And even more than that." She winked at him.

"I think hearing that is the best Christmas gift I could ever hope for."

"I'm just glad you're not on the harvester."

"I'll stop for Christmas, and with you here, I can make it a break for the entire day."

"A farmer's Christmas, then?"

"Well, some jobs still need to be done like feeding the alpacas. They like the extra bit of feed they get for Christmas, you know, especially Evie."

"She does like her food."

"So, do you."

"Hey." She playfully slapped him on the arm. He laughed.

"Merry Christmas." He handed her his gift.

She noticed Ben was holding his breath as she ripped the Christmas paper and lifted the lid of the box. "Are you saying I need to work more?" She lifted out one of the new work boots.

"Dammit, I should've just got you chocolate."

"I love them."

"What?"

"I need a pair of work boots if I'm staying. So, you're happy if I stay, right?"

"Damn right, I am."

"Good." She reached over and took out a small box. "Merry Christmas."

"You didn't need to get me anything."

"It's our first Christmas together. I wanted to."

He tore away the red and gold Christmas paper and picked up a little statue of an alpaca.

"It's too cute, right?" Raven squirmed. *He doesn't like it.*

"It reminds me of Evie."

"It's meant to."

Ben turned and put his arm around Raven, pulling her close to him. "Thank you." He kissed her long and slow. She sighed pleasantly.

"It will always remind me how much you've given up being here with me, to give us a chance."

She pecked him on the cheek. "This is my home now. I can feel it."

He brushed a wayward strand of hair from her face. "I'm so glad you feel that way."

"I love you," she kissed him, letting her mind spin with desire when their lips touched.

"I love you, too."

Raven shimmied closer to Ben, and they held each other, looking out at the farm, alpacas grazing in the paddock beyond the sheds.

"This wasn't how I thought Christmas would be, but I can honestly say it's perfect," said Raven.

"It is, and I look forward to many more with you. Maybe next year we'll manage to get a Christmas tree."

"With or without a Christmas tree, as long as you're with me, and we're here on the farm. I quite like this farmer's Christmas."

"Welcome to the family." Ben kissed her on the cheek. Raven smiled at him. It was good to finally feel like this was her home.

THE END

If you enjoyed this story, you may also like:

. . .

The Royal Show Affair
Click here to purchase
If you liked this story, you may also like:
Best in Show
Click here to purchase
A Country Christmas
Click here to purchase
Chasing Dust Clouds
Click here to purchase
A Dusty Christmas
Click here to purchase

Like urban paranormal romance?
Check out these books by Lilliana Rose
Protector Wolf Shifter Series
Bk1: Shadow Wolf
Bk2: Marked Wolf
Bk3: Rogue Wolf
Dragon Bond
Dragon Reborn
Witch Moon Series
Bk1: Dark Moon Secrets

ACKNOWLEDGMENTS

Thank you Kaylene for always having time to offer support and advice.

Thanks to my sisters for their support of their crazy sister who is a writer, and my toddler boy for being well-behaved so I can still have time to write and nurture my soul.

Thanks to my dog, Kimba, for reminding me when it's time to eat and go to bed, and for simply just lying there next to me or at my feet, being that extra life in the room, so the writing journey isn't so lonely.

ABOUT THE AUTHOR

Lilliana Rose is an Amazon Bestselling author, who writes romance in the subgenres of contemporary, paranormal, and rural. She enjoys helping characters overcome problems, or issues, and the misunderstandings that often plague relationships, to help them fall in love. Whether it city heels being replaced with country work boots, or some magic beyond this world, each story shows how love can prevail. She has over fifteen years' experience in various education systems as a teacher, a skip and a jump from starting out in genetics research. It is all helpful for inspiring her writing. She has poetry, middle grade, picture book, novellas and novels published under various pen names.

Check out more of her work at www.lillianarose.com.

Connect with her on social media.